Killer Tum Screaming Bloody Murder iN The BaSemeNt Of HeLL

...aNd OtHer StOries

bY CubeSVille

Killer Tunes and Screaming Bloody Murder in the Basement of
Hell ...and other stories

by
Cubesville

Copyright © Cubesville 2020

Second edition published in 2020 by Active
www.activedistribution.org

Tuesday is not Soylent Green Day first published in One Way
Ticket to Cubesville bumper comp (2018)

Record rarities: Shit on Society, Society's Lies EP first
published in One Way Ticket to Cubesville zine #20 (2017)

British Library Cataloguing in Publication Data

Cubesville
Raging Killer Tunes

ISBN13: 978-1-8380835-0-2

Author contact: cubesville@hotmail.com

CONTENTS

Side A

Side B

"I haven't fucked with the past, but I've fucked plenty with the future"

Patti Smith

INtrOduciNg...

First we'll spoil the ending: In each of these stories, the band got back together. Every time. Whatever the situation, whoever the protagonist, wherever they found themselves - on the other side of the universe, in the middle of an existential crisis, in a job they hate, sheltering from a zombie apocalypse, running away from a crap marriage, or still living with their mum, the stars always align and they get the band back together.

Do they live happily ever after? Chances are they weren't happy before, so they'll probably live more happy ever after - that's after they got the band back together. If that makes sense.

When life is so unrewarding, so desperate, so monotonous, or so bleak, is it really such a great leap backwards when you decide you're going to revitalise that crappy band that no-one remembers? Can anyone blame you for saying, "Fuck it," and that you want to spend time with like-minded people (with whom you may have fallen-out or from whom you grew apart) or just be creative despite the world's efforts to shut you up? Don't we all need to stop sometimes to put some meaning back into life? To make life feel good again?

That's why bands get back together, right?

THE REUNION REVOLUTION
Since around the start of the millennium, getting the band back together became a thing. It became normal. And if we're talking numbers, most reunions haven't been motivated by fame or fortune.

Away from the likes of The Pixies, or tearless, joyless reunions like The Sex Pistols, there are thousands of people whose social and economic conditions led them to reassert some kind of cultural output (rather than being prisoners in the worker/consumer cycle), and to take back control of their lives.

Their motive for getting the band back together has often been a great, yawning disappointment in what society offered

but didn't deliver. You know the sort of thing; life reneging
on its its promises of a golden future, employers welching
on the work ethic, career aspirations trampled into the mud,
frustrated people painting themselves into dark corners,
failed experiments at being grown-up, deferred dreams
coagulating at the bottoms of kitchen pedal bins or brave,
imaginative, far-thinking people flunking the challenge of
being normal.

That sort of thing.

I mentioned The Pixies and Sex Pistols before: when they
got their bands back together, many people who went to see
their second incarnations did so because they missed out
on their back-in-the-day performances. But in these stories
I've explored things from the perspective of the lost band or
forgotten band member. People for whom the veil was lifted,
and their innocent eyes saw that work, marriage, home, life, or
whatever distracted them from the band, just wasn't worth it.

So they got the band back together.

Why wouldn't you want to play a small gig in the back room
of a pub if it meant you were in the company of people who
actually cared about what you had to say?

Why not? Shouldn't we stop pretending to be the people that
the world wants us to be? Trying to meet the expectations of
a life-partner you'll never please? Why not find where your
heart really lies? Why not just get the band back together?

I tackle the tricky subject of nostalgia from a DIY punk
perspective. Given the choice of watching a reformed ageing
punk band, or standing in the aforementioned empty back room
of a scruffy pub while a contemporary act thrashes it out, for
me the here and now wins every time. Even if everyone else is
down the road enjoying the band that just got back together.
I can't help it - I never got into music to be on the winning
side. I was raised on the John Peel show on BBC radio. Peel
compared music to football, claiming that he was more
interested in that Saturday's scores than remembering past
glories. Having said that, the wistful, nostalgic theme tune

to his legendary show was a track called Pickin the Blues by
southern US rockers Grinderswitch; itself a cover of an older
blues artist. Nostalgia is a many-headed beast. And nostalgia
has some damn good tunes under its belt.

But this isn't about what the audience thinks, it's about the
band.

And this collection of short stories brings together different
voices in that revelation that they didn't make the right life
choices, or that society cheated them; that the world can go to
hell and fuck it, they're getting the band back together.

So join me in these absurd adventures, twisted tales, tear-
jerkers and apocryphal accounts. I promise you anarchy,
absurdity, and plenty of, errrm, getting the band back together.

MaSteRS Of The UNiVeRSe

We catch up with one of the great "lost bands", Sludgecake, following their extensive tour of Ptyx. Are they looking forward to playing their home town after all these (light) years?

The crowds were amazing. It's like that scene in the first Star Wars - you know, the one in the bar with all these different species with tentacles and fur and bug-eyes and stuff, but times a thousand. We started off with the set from the Cold Stoned Sober era and threw in a couple of covers - Ramones, Nirvana, The Inedibles, that kind of stuff - and Ptyx crowds were loving it. A set lasted as long as you liked, so in the early days we'd do a half hour or so until we progressed as musicians and developed a longer live set.

Sorry, I'm getting ahead of myself. You asked why have we got the band back together? Interesting question. The short answer is that we never split up. You're probably thinking of the line-up that released the Cold Stoned Sober EP. But at that time there were two versions of Sludgecake - a four-piece of the original members minus bassist Pug, and an alternate version which Pug formed with a few of his drinking mates.

Yeah, Pug's version had a much higher profile and gigged in the UK and Europe. But our version, the true Sludgecake, has gigged all this time. And much, much further afield. We've just celebrated our 26th anniversary together, released 13 studio albums and played in front of thousands of people. I know. Nobody here has heard of us apart from Japanese record collectors seeking original copies of that first EP.

We've been all over. I know. But let's take it back OK? Well, the original five-piece practised in a garage off Matthews Lane. This guy we called D-Tox owned it and he ran it as a "studio". It was really a lock-up on the edge of an industrial estate, which he'd sound-proofed with egg boxes and old mattresses. You could make a pretty good demo on a four-track in that room. It's where we recorded the Cold Stoned Sober EP, or what would become the Cold Stoned Sober EP when that moron Pug got left behind and had it cut by a record-pressing plant.

We'd been going about 18 months with the stable line-up of Davy and Ken on guitars, me on drums and Roddy singing. Yeah sorry, and Pug on bass. He was a proper knobhead though and only got in on the original line-up because he and Davy lived out in the sticks and they'd share a lift in together. Honestly, in 18 months he never progressed. If anything, he got less musical. He looked like a shaven-headed version of Sid James, you know the guy off the Carry On films. But not as handsome. We'd crank Davy's guitar right up to hide the fact that he couldn't play. In fact, Ken wasn't much cop back then in the early days - he got better later on when he switched to bass.

We'd just played Battle of the Bands and we'd lined up a few out-of-town gigs - Leeds, Liverpool and London with some grebo band. Phoenix Firm won the competition, but we went down pretty well considering we were the only punk band in the line-up. Well, we took a break from practising and Pug pulled out the beers - he and Davy had steady jobs so they were good for that at least.

There was a doorway at the back of the studio, which D-Tox usually kept locked. We always joked that it was where D-Tox kept his porn collection. But on that day I tried it and it opened.

And that was a doorway to a new life. On the other side there was this room about the same size as the studio, but filled with this machinery that looked like a 1950s computer - you know all valves and tape reels and that. Me, Davy and Roddy went in to have a look. "What the fuck's D-Tox building in here?" Roddy asked. "Is he some kind of Bond villain or something?" We laughed about it and made some bad impersonations of Blofeld - you know the one with the cat in You Only Live Twice, "We have discovered your porn collection Mr Bond - your Razzle and your Fiesta. Interesting Mr Bond."

But then we heard Ken behind us. "You would call it alien technology," he said. We turned round and I'm not joking, Ken had turned purple. Fucking purple. And he had these two antennae protruding from his forehead and they were wiggling about.

Well, we were pissing ourselves laughing at him and Davy went, "Ken you twat." Ken was just standing there straight-faced, while I was rolling around on the floor unable to breathe.

"It's a navigation system," Ken said, "a portal across the universe if you like." Well I didn't know about Ptyx (pronounced as a single click of the tongue) travel at the time and to be honest, it did look a bit ropey. Ken continued, unphased by our hilarity. "I've been looking for one of these to get me off this shithole of a planet since the MoD captured my crewmates," he said. "Let's crank this thing up and get out of here." Roddy, who had begun to take him seriously was like, "Really? You can get us out of Southport?"

"Mate, if I can get this working, I can take you to places that'll blow your mind. Get your instruments - we're off."

So that was it - we get our gear and cram it into the room while Ken tinkers with the knobs and buttons on this machine. Next thing we know, each of us experiences a loud humming inside our heads and everything looks a bit wobbly. Roddy says it's like he's gone through a bag of Evo.

Until then, I'd not taken Ken seriously but now I'm kind of shitting myself. I shout above the humming in my head: "Hang on, we're never going to see Southport again. What about all our mates and families? What about the gigs we've got lined up?"

"Fuck Southport," Roddy yells back at me, "fuck living in this shitheap. Fuck taking crap off trendies every day in this miserable fucking place. And fuck not getting into pubs cos we don't wear the right clothes. Fuck not having anything to do during the day. Fuck signing-on, and fuck people looking down their noses cos you're signing on, and fuck people telling you that you'll never get a job or make anything of your life looking like this, or ever get a girlfriend looking like this. And fuck people slagging you off cos you're in a band, or that your band just makes a racket, or that they know someone who's in a better band, or that you're wasting your life." All the while he's saying this, he's symbolically sticking two fingers up at the doorway. "Fuck," Roddy concludes, "Southport."

Davy's proper crapping it though, "It's alright for you Roddy," he yells, "but I've got a job and I don't want to lose it."

Ken turns to him, "The work you do in that bathroom fittings firm amounts to nothing," he says. "The future's bleak for you Davy - you'll never amount to much, although you'll kid yourself that you have. You'll find yourself stuck on the hamster wheel, wishing for something more but without the wherewithal to do anything about it. Eventually you'll hit 40 and start wishing you could backpack across Australia, win the Lottery, find a younger girlfriend or even get the band back together. Crushed and defeated, your conversation will revolve around what car you're driving at the moment, pointless and impotent conjecture about how your favourite football team - Liverpool isn't it - could improve their performance with some spending in the summer transfer window, or how you bought your house just at the right time. Your life, Davy, will be a pointless waste and your only discernable function on this planet will to be to make somebody you've never met and never likely to meet far richer, contented and fulfilled than yourself, while whichever equally confused, lost individual who agreed to share their life with you becomes steadily more impoverished, dissatisfied and disappointed in you."

"Wow Ken," Davy says, "you can see the future?"

"You were just born mediocre," Ken replies. "You come with me and we'll explore the stars together."

"Bollocks," Davy shouts, "fuck off Southport - space, here we come." We're yelling at Ken to crank up the portal and shouting "fuck Southport", which Roddy would fashion into a lyric and would become Sludgecake's closing number for a while, when Davy goes, "Shit, what about Pug? We've forgotten him."

"Even by earth standards," Ken replies, "Pug is a total knobhead. He's racist, sexist and homophobic. He has an IQ the level of a baboon, which, coincidentally, matches both his bass-playing ability and his sexual prowess. Southport deserves him, and he deserves Southport."

"Fair point," Davy goes. "What a knob." Everything's humming and spinning by now, and it looks like we're off. Through the still-open door we see Pug appear with a can of beer in his hand and a bemused frown on his sloping forehead.

We thought afterwards that he was calling out for us to stop or to take him with us, but it all got a bit hazy really. I haven't spoken to him since we got back, but I believe he's still living in Southport. Probably still drinking with the same bunch of Neanderthals as when we left. I dunno - I'm not going back there, it would be too depressing really. After we left, Pug got together with a couple of mates and called themselves Sludgecake - he even took the credit for writing the songs on the Cold Stoned Sober demo, which he stuck out as an EP.

But to be honest, he had no musical talent and his version of the band was even more generic than before. I think there were even some far-right connection, but don't quote me on that. It wouldn't surprise me though. Yeah, I can understand he'd be upset with us for leaving him behind and if he's reading this, could you say that we didn't mean him any harm really. We saw a chance to get out of Southport and seized the moment. He would have done the same.

The other side of the portal? Fucking amazing mate. Why do you think we were out there for so long?

Well, Ptyx is a term for this enormous, sprawling collective of species and planets who pooled their know-how into developing ways of, kind of travel, but without the flying saucers. Ken's crew were the exception and were captured when they got to Earth. He was lucky to have escaped - his crewmates were taken to Aldershot I think and never reappeared.

Ptyx stretches across galaxies, and that big 1950s computer thing was a doorway or a nodal point which is joined to the next and the next and so on. Like a big spider's web. That's why Fermin's Theory is so flawed - the one that says if there was intelligent life on other planets, we would have seen it by now. We're just looking in the wrong place, and in the wrong way - the answer's right under our noses.

So we enter Ptyx and that's when it really takes off for us. Ptyx travels great distances and has resolved a lot of those difficult interfaces between different species, or in some cases different phyla, so it's pretty friendly on the whole. And when you want, you can jump to a different nodal point. Just like that. We needed to be useful to the collective, so we played as a touring band.

Ken switched over to bass - yeah, we did feel bad about taking Pug's bass, but he would have done the same to us. And the band improved straight away. Not that it mattered really. The prospect of a band from Earth was so novel to much of Ptyx that we could have been playing anything really. Like when the Berlin Wall came down and random Western bands toured Eastern Europe. You had some real shite going over in the early days, but they were well-received in places like Prague or Brno because people hadn't seen a UK or US band before.

Well, that's the funny thing, we weren't the only Earth band in on the game. Of course, Ptyx is vast, so you're going from gig to gig all the time, but you bump into other bands once in a while. Yeah - Iron Maiden were our favourites, and Bruce Dickinson was loving the space travel thing. Let's see - The xxxxxx, xxxxx xxxx, xxxx of the xxx xxxxx were some of the names you might know. And some big names too - remember Japan? Or Banarama? These bands didn't split up, they just toured Ptyx.

We heard that U2 attempted to buy their way into Ptyx, but even species that existed in relative isolation without the cultural reference points or the sensory equipment to properly assimilate the same dimensional make-up relative to the people on the stage could see that they were shite. They fully recognised that Bono was a total chancer and an utter wanker - he even tried to undermine the collective harmony of Ptyx and introduce free market economics. What a knob. Crowds like alkja8u totally bottled them off so they had to return to Earth.

They totally loved us though, and we made a point of going back to alkja8u every orbit to play to each successive generation as they hatched. Regular gig for us that.

Musically, I think you'd describe what we were doing as post-rock. We wrote-off Cold Stoned Sober when we learnt how to play. With hindsight, having Pug in the band was holding us back even then. But Ken moving to bass really worked for us.

And when he transitioned, it really improved our stage presence.

Transitioning? Yeah, well Ken was actually from an arachnid planet located in the Ptyx collective, and his human form was a larval stage. Spiders from Mars, if you like. When we first met him in Southport, he was a juvenile, and even the purple thing that set us off laughing in the practice studio was a stage in his development.

We were wrong to laugh at him, and he's been really good about it. You wouldn't recognise him now. He retained what we'd call hands, so playing the bass isn't a problem, but he sprouted another four legs, and he now has composite eyes like an insect. The band was pretty good about all that - we made sure that each venue we played could physically accommodate him and they could cater for his changing dietary requirements, especially those enormous beetle things. And that he had proper sleeping quarters so he could hang upside down from the ceiling.

Well, he's a mate and we're all really close - both as a band and as a group of friends. We've come a long way together.

I've heard that some Earth bands have been freaked out by some of the species they met in Ptyx, but I reckon coming from a conservative town like Southport actually made us more open-minded towards all that. I really like the cosmopolitan atmosphere around the portals, with loads of different species mixing together. And the food is magnificent. Yeah, I think back to Roddy saying "fuck Southport" all those years ago and I think of how lucky we were to get out of there.

Well, while we were in Ptyx we notched up thousands of gigs, and we even found a space on an android satellite we could use as a studio. We would pop over there every few Earth years to record an album. Most of Ptyx lives in the here-and-now, so they aren't interested in recorded music, but we found a ready audience among The Librarians - they live on this crazy planet full of books, and are totally obsessed with archiving absolutely everything.

So, yeah, we made 13 proper studio albums and did a couple of live albums. Just to have a record of what we'd done really. You can hear the progression - taking on jazz influences and exploring ambient sounds with bits of electronica here and there.

We even guested a few musicians from across Ptyx. My favourite was from an underwater race, who made this frantic bubbling sound. Honestly, you've got to listen to it - we laid down a kind of dub track behind it - it's crazy.

Why did we come back to Earth? Yeah good question. Well, we were all getting on a bit I suppose. And we'd been touring solidly for more than 20 years; your body can't take the constant gigging, late nights and portal-hopping as well as it can when you're younger.

I heard that's why Andrew Ridgely gave up that phenomenal solo career he built up in Ptyx after Wham!. Plus I think Roddy and Davy wanted to breed with their own species before they got too old. I'm not fussed to tell you the truth.

Yeah it would be a good opportunity to show the world what happened to Sludgecake in the intervening years and that the Cold Stoned Sober EP isn't indicative of the sound that we developed while we were out in Ptyx.

Ken? Yes, he's still with us. Well, we couldn't split the band up just because we returned to Earth. And when we found out how much the Cold Stoned Sober EP has been sought-after by record collectors, it opened up all kinds of opportunities for us on the reunion circuit. Even though we've been together all this time so it's not technically a reunion.

Yeah, I reckon Ken's arachnid form will turn a few heads, but that's all the better for us really.

17

I suppose the downside is that the rest of the band has to go out and seek food for him, but that's what mates are for. And that's the lucky thing about being back on Earth - the closest we found to his natural food is actually human beings. Yeah, we only have to catch a couple a month to keep him going, and then get rid of the skins afterwards. He seems quite happy with the arrangement and it's good to have him here with us.

Would you like to meet him? Yeah, no problem he's just in the other room. Yeah, just leave your stuff there and don't worry about the coffee mug - we'll clear that up afterwards.

Just through this door... Come on... Don't be shy...

The Day The World Stood Still

In which our protagonist is called into the office - receives some unwelcome news - gets drunk if the afternoon - yep, gets the band back together. Set sometime around 2010 when the bosses were really taking the piss. Piss-taking bastard bosses.

"I suppose you're wondering," Gareth has had his hair cut again, "why we've called you in this morning." Not that it's made any difference. Often, you can tell a person's age by how dated their appearance is. It's like carbon-dating them. Back to when they stopped making an effort and stayed with what they thought looked cool, or appeared presentable. Or it became too much effort to change.

Jackie and Paul Robinson for example. Jackie is all about big hair and shoulder pads, while Paul Robinson wears his hair slightly longer at the back like he had a splendid mullet way back in the day, cascading down the shoulders of his blouson denim jacket. Or tasselled suede coat. Whatever. Both gave up caring in their early 20s. They act like they've been married for years. Even though Paul Robinson has a wife and grown-up kids. Sitting opposite each other every day. Both standing up at 12-30pm sharp and setting off for lunch together. Not speaking, but communicating through some psychic link that excludes the rest of us. I got told Paul Robinson was in the SAS, but nobody's ever asked him about it. He looks like he probably was. Him and Jackie just get left to get on with it.

Gareth's much younger. "They only call me Gary the once," he said when I first started at this place. He gave up at the turn of the noughties. He probably thought Offspring were cool when he was a teenager, dancing around to them in front of the telly. His gateway band sort of thing. He's got this thing going on that I call "the clasp" - a fringe that sticks upwards so he looks like Tintin. Hair smeared with product so the rest of it is plastered down like a helmet. Greasy Gary. If you threw a pen at it, would it bounce off or stick to the

19

gel? I'd put a fiver on it sticking to the gel. I'm guessing he's mid/late 30s - you know when they make a go of their career. Insufferable to the rest of us. There isn't a line on his boyish face, like he hasn't suffered in life.

He told me he'd been with the company for 15 years, which is about right. He'd have sat there trying to get noticed for five of those, and a step up the ladder every three or four years after that. It's an age-old story about potential middle manager joins company. Big ideas. Going places. They stop all that by the time they get to my age. I had my 15 minutes when the powers that be wanted to know what I thought - requested my input when they overhauled the Corporate Social Responsibility Policy. Or got me to report back from conferences in Dublin, Dubai or Doncaster. Travel did my head in. And I hated the hotels.

But for the last five years, I've been left to rot. Mundane tasks, no responsibility, no direction. Fair play, no motivation on my part. If I had any get-up-and-go, I'd have called in HR and got someone, Greasy Gary probably, done for workplace bullying. Or the union. Left under a cloud - tribunal pending. A few home truths and slammed the door on the way out. Which is what Jo did.

Not here, but at home. Which I totally regret. Before the rot, she was pestering me to do something with my life. Something that wasn't the boring end of retail. Something that didn't leave me washed-out and just so defeated by it all. But I only took this job to put food on the table for us while she went off and did her yoga instructor's course. I thought I was doing the decent thing - letting Jo go off and follow her dreams. Have a rewarding, inspiring life while I sorted out what I wanted to do with mine. With ours. She even went to a retreat in India.

And one outside Carlisle. Of course I worried that we were growing apart. And I sat there stewing over what she got up to at these yoga retreats. But it was one of her students she went off with. Stayed local, which added insult to injury. Property Management Consultant (read: Estate Agent), 10 years her junior. Thinks of himself as a free spirit - hippie type.

Money is like an energy, channelled along my flippin chakras or whatever. All pantaloons, hemp shirts and sandals outside of office hours. Hair tied up in a bun. A man-bun. Fuck's sake.

Funds Jo's yoga school. Feel Free Yoga. Thirty-something suburban mummies, tantric sexual predators, recovering alcoholics and a few crazies thrown in for good measure. "Running Feel Free Yoga," her website reads, not that I've been cyber-stalking her, "allows me to do what I've always wanted - to be a free spirit, and free from a regular office job." A quick root round Companies House confirmed, for me at least, that Feel Free Yoga was a vanity business funded by the Estate Agent, who is company director, and also director of their suburban yoga retreat.

I didn't dwell on the controlling nature of his being company director. Or the appearance of another director's name, Melody. I stayed with my theory that Estate Agent was happy to fund the vanity business to counter the massive burden of guilt he must carry around, what with making a living by screwing ordinary people every day.

"We established our healing yoga retreat," claims the website, "to deepen your understanding and establish a place of self discovery through the four energy system's of yoga." Free spirit Estate Agent didn't tell her there's no apostrophe in "systems". Come to think of it though, it reads like it was written by an estate agent.

I'm guessing she's happier just to get on with the teaching part of it. Weekends of silence and undercooked vegetables. Which sounds like life in our flat towards the end of our relationship. But not in a hatha way. Can you actually weave yoghurt? Mung beans - surprisingly, I'm for them. Despite my comment about undercooked vegetables, Jo made a killer mung daal when we were together. Great stuff. Her signature dish. And plenty left over for the next day. So don't believe the stereotype - mung beans are great stuff.

"Are you actually," Christ, it's Gareth. Totally drifted off there, "listening to me?"

He's donned his concerned frown - one of his two expressions, alongside that shit-eater grin. Like he just realised that he'd squeezed a tube of haemorrhoid cream onto his toothbrush by mistake and had brushed his teeth with it. And bloody hell, he's actually telling me off like I'm a naughty schoolboy.

Sue from HR is in the room with us today. She's tapping away at her laptop computer. Sacker Sue, wearing the same frown as Greasy Gareth. Her other expression is the shit-eater grin. Do they send them on a course or something? Make them sit there grinning till they've got it right? Before they escort them down to the car park to drill them in the company goose step.

"Sure I am Gareth," I reply, looking lively, "you were about to tell me why you've got me here this morning." The pair of them watch me for a few moments, so I fill the silence: "Am I in for a bollocking or something?" I fell into that one, they made me speak first. Turned it round on me - they invited me to the meeting, so it's up to them to do the talking. I just have to sit here and not say or do anything too outlandish.

"Do," Gareth breaks the silence, "you think you deserve a bollocking?" Concerned frowns from Gareth and Sacker Sue. I say nothing, just sit there blinking at them and wait for them to speak. Easy this. "Well, it's not good news this morning I'm afraid," he continues. "As you probably know, we've been experiencing a challenging market, and we have legacy issues associated with the merger. But as you may have read in the shareholders' report, we've got through most of that now, with a streamlined business focussing on our core markets and cornerstones of," this part always makes me laugh, "Customer-focussed, Respectful, Attentive and Personable." Yep, cornerstones of C-R-A-P. I'm squirming and trying not to laugh.

How the hell did that one get through marketing? It's like their mental health initiative, Caring, Understanding, Talking, No-shame. C-U-T-N. So very close. "Even though we can see the light at the end of the tunnel, and it's been a long journey for all of us, we're still not in the clear." Mixed metaphors. Corporate metaphor salad if you like. Or a metaphor buffet. A metaphor thingy... a smorgasbord of tired metaphors. An endless, all-day metaphor breakfast. The full-English metaphor. "And it is with some regret that we have to review your position with us." Keep listening - nearly lunch. "I'm sure you appreciate it has been a hard decision to make and understand that to ensure the sustainability of our business, we have reviewed everyone's position within the company." Why the hell call a meeting so close to noon? None of us can concentrate round this part of the day - we're all thinking of food. Let's get through this, slope off for lunch and then ride out the afternoon. "So it is our duty to inform you that your job is under consultation."

"Sorry, could you repeat that Gareth? I didn't catch what you were saying."

This is when Sue leans into the conversation. Concerned frown. "Your job is under consultation," she tells me. "As part of the redundancy process." Sacker Sue.

I would like to think I grabbed Gareth by the lapels and told him what I thought of him. Told him to stuff his job. But as you can guess, that didn't happen. Instead, I just sat there and stared at them both. "It must be a lot to take in," Sacker tells me. "We both understand if you need to take time to reflect."

"Obviously," Grease-ball continues, "it will mean a time of upheaval - both for you on a personal level, and for us as a company. Going forwards, your job will be shared among the remaining team, but how we plan to implement this is still under discussion. In the meantime, we fully understand if you would like to use your remaining annual leave."

So I stood up, extended my hand for Gareth to shake. I think I did that just to show them both I wasn't hurt by what they were doing to me. And I left. No argument. No final show-down. No "Stick your job up your arse and fuck off when you've done it." Nothing. I felt dead inside.

I walked out into a busy city centre on a Friday lunchtime. People, working people, went about their business, heedless that I may have walked among them, but I no longer belonged with them.

They probably couldn't tell just by looking at me that I
wasn't an economically active working person. I was no
longer employed. Like Monty Python's dead parrot, my gainful
employment had passed on! This worker was no more! His
contract had ceased to be! He had been retired and gone to meet
his maker (or the Department of Work and Pensions). Bereft
of job, 'e loafs around in peace! My economic activity was now
'istory! THIS WAS AN EX-WORKER!!

So I drifted through the crowd. I wasn't angry yet, just
completely shell-shocked.

I'd become so settled into this stupid job that I didn't like and
I couldn't imagine losing the meagre salary I got from it. It
was like I'd become scared of the outside world.

The contract was pants and wouldn't give me much redundancy
to go on - probably the barest minimum required by law. Those
tight-fisted bastards. And all that fanfare they make about
Corporate Social Responsibility and putting people first.
Horse shit.

Savings would probably see me through five months if nothing
terrible happened. Which was a relief. I could eke that out
a bit further with a few economies on my already Spartan
lifestyle. Not switching the heating on until November and
living on sodding mung beans. Bloody whatsit, hatha yoga
instead of telly. So I wasn't out on the street just yet. What
the hell had I left in my desk? Anything incriminating? I
couldn't remember.

And this meeting must have been brewing for some time. Like,
had Greasy been waiting for us to get through a pile of work
before sacking me? Do you call it sacking? Never mind all that
"refocussing the business on our core values of sodding People,
Opportunity and Outstanding-value", or POO!

Yeah, "Heads of Delivery, Innovation and Corporate Knowledge-
base," or DICK Heads! This must have been on the cards for a
while. And what can you do about it? Employers aren't obliged
by law to give you a job, and yet they have plenty of slack to
get rid of you whenever the fancy takes them. Can't they warn

us so we can look for something else? In the old days, I kept
a union membership, but that lapsed when the rot set in - I
thought I'd save a few quid a month and I held the job in such
low regard that I didn't think it mattered if they fired me.
But now they had. So there.

I gravitated towards a pub I'd started to frequent after Jo left
- The Ship. The Ship was a nice, old-school pub, with a cool
selection on the jukebox. The people who drank there really
knew their music and the place had a nice vibe to it. I first
went when Stu was still working with us, before his operation.
Since then, I fell into the habit of popping in on Fridays.

After Jo walked out, sorry, pursued a different path along the
four energy systems of yoga - disloyalty, infidelity, getting-
out-while-the-going-was-good and the highest fucking Chakra
or Hatha of all; lying-through-your-fucking-teeth - I got back
into drinking.

Jo was going through recovery when we met - booze and Class
A drugs - so I reined it right in to accommodate that. She was
on some kind of journey even back then, and the yoga was the
next step. She had been into cool music, like indie and goth,
but some of the folks from that scene got her into heavy stuff.
Like smack from what she told me. I knew her from gigs, but I
was more of a pub man, and I didn't have any truck for drugs.
Which held us together. For a brief chapter of our lives. Held
together by what you don't do. Held together by what you're not.

The Dancing Man was smoking a cigarette in the doorway. He
drank in The Ship during the afternoon with an older crowd
who all sloped off at teatime. The Dancing Man wouldn't let
you past him unless you danced with him. Smoke-shrivelled
face, drainpipe trousers and a glorious Roy Orbison wig. What
the hell was his story?

"No," I said as he flipped up the collar of his leather coat and
gyrated his ageing pelvis like if Elvis hadn't keeled over from
a heart attack while sitting on the toilet back in 1977 and
had settled down to drinking steadily and solidly in The Ship
ever since.

I would like to think Elvis is still out there somewhere, just getting on with his life without the world pecking his fucking head all the time. "Just no," I said.

"Smile son," The Dancing Man replied as he stepped aside to let me through, "you get yourself a drink. Keep smiling son."

There was space at the end of the bar, so I dragged over a stool and settled in for a session. I didn't want to go home by myself, and who was I going to call to talk about what they'd done to me at work? Phoning Jo would be just weird. During our time together, I'd drifted away from my regular crowd, and I couldn't think of anyone I'd burden with this crap. No-one at all.

It was Smiley Samantha's shift on the bar, which lifted my mood. Twenty-something, piercings, tats, big smile, treated you like an equal, a human being in fact, and importantly she remembered what you drank. I didn't want to talk about today, or even think about that crap earlier on with Greasy and Sacker.

So I stared at nothing and had a few beers, which made me feel lots better. Every now and again, The Dancing Man and his cronies would come up to the bar to blow more of their disability benefit, or pension, or wherever they got the cash to drink in that pub every single afternoon without fail, and I'd exchange pleasantries with them.

The Dancing Man put a few quid into the jukebox. He selected a few old rock and roll classics - you know, Roy Orbison, Carl Perkins, Johnny Cash, that sort of thing - and swaggered round the bar singing and dancing to them. In a funny way, he was just the tonic I needed - a world away from Greasy and Sacker. I made sure to buy him and the cronies a whiskey each to thank them.

Towards late afternoon, a young rock dude came in to prop up the bar. He knew Sam and they talked about some gig that he'd been to but she missed because she was working. Hearing them talk like that reminded me of being their age - skint most of the time, but ace people and ace social life. I wanted to know which gig it was, I wanted to be there.

Greasy and Sacker and all those other small minded people in that office - they never knew what these people had. How music is the social glue that holds us all together whatever and whoever we are. The Dancing Man and Sam and me and rock dude. We got it.

I got chatting to rock dude, Ashley. He said he was waiting for the coach down to Bristol and he asked me if I played pool. I told him not in a while, but I gave him a game. From his prowess at the pool table, I'd have said Ashley was commendably misspending his youth. I made sure he had a drink in his hand for the few games we played together. After we finished, he insisted on buying us a Jaegerbomb each. We parted as friends and he made his way to the coach station.

Sam's boyfriend Dan was at the bar when I resumed my place, and ordered another pint. We got chatting straight away; Dan was having trouble finding work on the festival circuit, which he blamed on the recession.

"Tell me about it," I said, "they're laying people off left, right and centre. I'm going through a redundancy myself at the moment."

"Ah, tough one dude," Dan replied, and offered me a drink.

I bought him one while I still could and we put a couple of quid into the jukebox. We hummed and hawed over the selection; I wasn't familiar with what he chose, but he was impressed with my selection of The Cult and The Mission.

"You like that old goth stuff then?" He asked with genuine enthusiasm.

I told him it was the stuff of my youth, and added that I spent some time playing in a band. Cthulhu Mythos. Originally we were Cthulhu Club - a jokey name as a reaction to Culture Club. But the others started taking themselves more and more seriously so we changed the name.

And we changed members when personalities clashed. And we changed musical direction a few times. And we changed the way

27

we looked. But interestingly, I was the longest-serving and only original member. Probably because I didn't fight with the others. Bass and guitar had equal weighting in that band, but I guess guitarists are always the ego-centric ones, while I, the bass guitarist, gave our songs atmosphere and texture without causing friction among my bandmates.

Towards the end, the singer, interestingly called Gary like my recent boss, assumed control of the band and dictated what we should play. We'd got quite big by then, at least in our world, and had some indie chart success and night-time radio play. Eventually Gary opted to go off in his own direction, and that's more or less the same time that I got together with Jo. So that was the end of Cthulhu Mythos and the beginning of a journey along a different path for me.

Dan and Sam were totally engrossed in my story. They asked about our records - three LPs - and gigs and tours we'd played. We even got on regional TV a couple of times. Dan had one of these flashy mobile phones that you could get the internet on. I know everyone has one these days, but he was well ahead of the pack. So with a bit of searching, he pulled up a photo of Cthulhu Mythos, and myself and Sam leant in to see if we could pick me out. And do you know what? The years hadn't been too unkind to me. OK, in the photo, my lanky hair was dyed raven black, and I still had cheekbones and pencil-thin legs, but you could see it was me. Standing there in the dry ice. My new friends were well impressed. Sam showed the picture to a few of the other drinkers, who gave their approval.

"Haven't you wanted to carry on making music?" Sam asked me. "You don't want to get up there and do it again?"

This had been the first time in years that I'd even thought of the band. It had been such a big part of my life, but when I drifted away from it, I hardly gave it a second thought. All I could reply to Sam was, "I just stopped doing it." What else could I say? Bore her about my break-up with Jo? About how the rot set in with work, and I became so uninspired and useless that even my employers spurned me? How do you describe the years of unrewarding existence? Institutionalised and trapped in a cage of your own making? How could I tell her I was hiding here in this pub, unceremoniously fired just earlier today, and I was here because I had nowhere to go and I was scared to face the outside world?

And then Dan dropped the bombshell, "You haven't considered getting the band back together?"

And for the first time in some years, Dan presented me with a way out. Another path; not the dead end that I had drifted into. A chance to do something inspiring, and something the rest of the world actually liked. People respected me. I had been the longest-serving member after all. Just imagine, doing something that people actually came along to see?

"Wow," I said, taken aback by the thought. "You've got me there. I suppose it would depend on Gary."

"You should do it," Sam said. "Why don't you give him a call?"

"Yeah," Dan agreed, "what have you got to lose? Especially with the redundancy - now could be the time."

"Do it," said Sam.

"Yeah man, do it," added Dan.

So I climbed down from the barstool and wobbled over to the public phone. I had Gary's number in the back of my diary, so I put some money in the slot and dialled his number. Despite the numbing effects of the pints and the Jaegerbomb, my heart pounded while I waited for Gary to pick up. Wouldn't he have moved on in life? Wouldn't getting the band back together sound a stupid idea? Especially as I was the one with the least musical input into it? That's why I'd survived so long. What kind of a fool was I about to make of myself?

Then I heard Gary's voice. "Hello?"

"Gary, its' me," I blurted. "It's me Gary. Been a long while. How are you man?"

After a moment's pause he recognised my voice. "Christ, this is a blast from the past," he said. "To what do I owe the pleasure? And where are you? It sounds like you're in the pub."

"I am mate," I replied. "Listen, I've got something to ask you. I've been talking to these kids and telling them all about Cthulhu Mythos. Anyway, they think it would be a good idea for us to get the band back together. A reunion like. You know, I'm just freelancing at the moment, so I've got some time on my hands. What do you say? I think the interest is out there."

While I was saying this, I could hear Gary chuckling on the other end of the phone. "How many have you had mate?" he asked. "Get the band back together! I'll have one of what you've been drinking. Classic. How's Jo and what does she say about this? Haven't you got a regular job to do?"

"Me and Jo aren't a couple any more," I told him. "And like I said, I'm freelancing at the moment, so I've got some time on my hands."

"Sorry to hear that," he said. "But I'll let you get back to your pint. Get the band back together. Classic mate. Brilliant. Just wait till I tell the others."

And that was it. I walked back to the barstool and slumped down. "Nothing doing," I said to my new friends.

"Tough," commiserated Dan. "But if he doesn't want to do it, it doesn't stop you from playing your old stuff. People will want to hear it, even if it's just you in the band."

"I dunno," I said, rejected and despondent. "I don't feel too good about it."

"We'll do it," Sam said. "Dan on keyboards, me on guitar?"

It sounded so simple. Put as enthusiastically as that, and with a drink in my hand, who cared about seeking Gary's approval? These people were up for it - they were a breath of fresh air after what life had dealt me recently - we could just have a bit of fun and enjoy it.

"Well," I mused. "I guess we could get a drum machine. Drummers are always difficult."

So Sam stood us a round of Jaegerbombs. And then I got one in. And Dan stood a round too. The rest of the night was a blur. I stayed round at Sam's on her couch after her and Dan helped me into a taxi. Apparently, Dave the landlord came down into the pub later on when it was busy to help out behind the bar, and I took exception to him because I'd overheard Sam and another bar worker, Amber I think, saying what an old perv he was. So when he started ordering Sam around I lost it with him. Told him to keep his hands to himself or he'd have me to contend with.

I felt really bad about that the next day, especially when Dave rang Sam to tell her that she wasn't needed for that night's shift. He spun her a story, just like Greasy and Sacker did to me the day before, about how business was dying and that that they'd divide her shifts with the other bar staff. I apologised, but Sam said she was impressed I'd stood up to him. Dan said it was really funny, and that they'd both been surprised by my massive mood swing. Must have been the Jaegerbombs - all that caffeine and alcohol sloshing around inside me. Especially as they sacked me right before lunch. Perhaps I'd seen enough of people being pushed around.

It's funny to look back on that now.

Greasy and Sacker giving me the boot was probably the best thing that could have happened. It saved me rotting in that job and moping around over Jo, and allowed me to get on with what I wanted to do.

Getting the band back together with Sam and Dan was just what my life needed. They were easy company and well-connected to get us plenty of gigs. We played all over the UK and Europe, and we were paid to go to the States where there were loads of fans who didn't get to see us the first time round.

Yeah, since then I've eked-out a precarious existence, but that's what I was doing anyway. And this way I'm not at the mercy of Greasy and Sacker who'd dismiss you at the drop of a hat. I heard Greasy Gareth got the boot six months after me in another streamlining, refocussing initiative. Those bastards have no loyalty - not even to goose steppers like Gareth. I do like to think, however, that it was Sacker Sue who told him his job was under review.

Jo succumbed to Estate Agent's deep yearning to be a father and became a 40-something mum. She blogs about yoga and motherhood and I dunno, weaving her own hemp yoghurt in the idyllic thatched cottage they moved out to. Blah, blah, blah, whatever. Move on.

I suppose when Greasy and Sacker called me in that morning, it was a lesson in how brittle life is, how unsteady the foundations on which we stand and something about how uncertain are our futures. But what I learnt was how the next chapter can just open up before us. And sometimes you first need a melt-down to allow you to get on with that next chapter.

Or was that the Jaegerbombs talking?

Killer Tunes aNd Screaming bloodY murder frOm The Basement Of Hell

In which our anti-hero survives a zombie apocalypse, reforms his powerviolence band, and maintains more or less the same pissed and stoned lifestyle he did before the world turned to crap. Not bad eh?

The facility had been on lock-down for a whole month before the new consignment of research specimens arrived from Manchester. Nothing had come in or gone out until the Colonel was sure the perimeter fence was absolutely safe again.

People were going stir-crazy holed up in the Centre, but at least I had my jam sessions with Jon to keep us both from losing it completely. Jon headed-up the research team and his way of unwinding involved battering the hell out of a drum kit he had stashed away down in the bunker.

By a stroke of luck, I procured a guitar and amp from the guys in Facilities Management; it was like old times with the two of us making noise together down there while the world above us went to ruin. Well, it would have been if we had Chas on board. More of that later.

And it had been a massive stroke of luck that got me safely behind the fence of the Better Understanding of Microbes Hub of Observation, Learning and Education (or to give the facility its correct acronym, BUMHOLE) Centre in the first place. I was among the first to be evacuated when the cities were overrun and the Government declared a State of Emergency. It all happened so fast that we hardly had time to respond.

Within days of the first reported case, the infection spread like wildfire and consumed the whole country. Within minutes, contamination of just a drop of infected body fluid would turn the victim into a red-eyed slavering murderer. The contagion tore through whole towns leaving their inhabitants dead, infected or, like me, fugitive.

I had been on tour with my stoner rock band, Bogus, when I first witnessed the devastating onset of the virus. We had just finished a dismal Monday night set at Manchester's Star and Garter, and were packing away our instruments. Even by our low standards the atmosphere in that place was flat that night.

The few people who did brave the weather to pay-in and watch us just stood there like zombies, and to be honest, they were only slightly less animated than the band. Both support bands had pulled out at the last minute, and we were obliged to drag our threadbare set out for an hour. I stood there looking at the bored faces in the crowd and felt genuinely sorry for people to have witnessed such a lacklustre delivery of an uninspired collection of dull songs. I'd like to say that is was not one of our finest performances, but if I'm truthful, it was pretty standard for Bogus.

Then, as I was putting my guitar back in its case, I heard Carlos shout something from behind his drum kit. I turned my head just in time to see him dragged off the stage by two maniac fans who looked hell-bent on tearing him apart. I stood there watching in disbelief, while all hell broke loose. People who had spent the last hour standing slack-mouthed and rooted to the beer-soaked dancefloor were now hurling themselves around the gig room; either in terror or with murderous intent. It took just a few moments for the whole place to turn into a bloodbath.

I hadn't time to properly process the pandemonium, but my survival instinct kicked right in and I got my arse into gear straight away. I knew my chance lay in getting to the beer cellar - I had been down there before the gig to pick up a mic stand (while pilfering a cheeky couple of cans of Red Stripe) and I knew it was unlocked. I tore down the stairs like shit off a shovel, right through that shrieking, snarling gorefest, slipping on blood and entrails, shaking off the desperate clasping hands of the dying and kicking out at the lurching, slavering Infected who barred my way to safety. OK, I didn't feel too great about locking the door behind me while there were other people to save, but as I slipped the bolt I reckoned the game was just about up for them anyway. And as I said, my survival instinct was in the driving seat, while the rest of me got comfortable and settled down for the ride.

The next week went by in a haze of bottled beer, spirits and bar snacks while I sat out whatever bedlam had broken out in the bar above. Thankfully, the venue had just taken a delivery from the brewery and it wasn't until a few days into my confinement that I was eventually reduced to breaking into the crates of Newcastle Brown Ale. It can't have been that bad judging by the empties and general wreckage I'd done to the place - I must have got a taste for Newcastle Brown towards the end.

Anyway, the next thing I knew, I was shaken awake by a militiaman who had broken into the beer cellar in search of supplies (the poor guy looked like he was spitting feathers). Seeing that I'd made a not insignificant hole in them, he decided to rescue me and pick up some commission. With a full-on whiskey-and-Newcastle-Brown hangover, I fled with him through the ruined streets of Manchester; the pair of us armed with the last of the Baileys and Sambuca.

It was terrifying to see the extent of the carnage - corpses and dismembered body parts were everywhere. And surveying the debris, there must have been savage pitched battles while I was holed-up back there in the beer cellar. An eerie quiet now hung over the city, which could be shattered at any moment as we picked our way across the devastation on that treacherous journey out into the Peak District and to the last safe refuge here at the Centre.

Thankfully, the Committee considered my day-job as an electrician to be useful enough to warrant a full-time place on the staff, and I immediately busied myself conducting portable appliance tests.

And who should be here leading the team that tirelessly worked to seek-out a cure for the apocalyptic virus? None other than former bandmate Jon; the powerhouse drummer in our cruelly short-lived powerviolence trio, Decimated Population.

While we were besieged behind the electric fence by the snarling, murderous hordes of Infected, Jon and I set to work converting a storeroom in the nuclear bunker below the Centre into a rehearsal room.

Beneath 18 inches of reinforced concrete, we made as much noise as we liked.

And when the militia brought Jon a new batch of research specimens, it gave our little sessions a new lease of life.

I was out by the generator shed having a crafty toke with Plumber Dave when I saw Jon running across the grounds; his enormous bulk gave him away, as did his wizard's beard, unmistakable white lab coat and loosely-tied ponytail, which all flailed in the wind behind him.

"Don't worry Dave, Jon's one of us," I assured my co-worker as I passed him the enormous steaming doobie I'd constructed earlier in my store cupboard.

"It's Chas!" my bandmate huffed, gasping for air after his run, "They've only gone and hauled in Chas." Chas! Chas the former frontman of our short-lived band. Chas, that charismatic teenager who had brought us together in the first place. I could hardly believe that Lady Luck had once again smiled on me. Despite the cruelty that filled the world around us, despite the constant state of terror in which we now lived, I was to be reunited with another old friend.

Just hearing the name of our former singer filled me with hope: Chas! Hope that somewhere out there were more survivors of the terrible plague that had ripped the world apart; hope that civilisation persisted beyond the electric fence and the stark grey utility buildings that we now called home; hope that Jon and his team would develop a vaccine that would save us all from this hell on earth; hope that mankind would have the strength to build a new world once all this was over. And above all else, an anxious, heart-pounding hope that now Chas was with us, the three of us could get the band back together.

"He's alive," I yelled jubilantly in Jon's face, "is he alright?"

"Not exactly," Jon replied, having regained his customary stoic manner, "he's one of them. He must have been bitten or something. We've got him locked up in the observation room. He's going bonkers. Come and see him, It really is Chas. He's hilarious!" Jon graciously accepted the joint proffered by Dave, and took a long appreciative draw on it till the end glowed as red as the eyes of the slavering murderous semi-humans on the other side of the electric fence.

"Sick," I said. "This I gotta see."

On the other side of the observation room's two-way mirror, was the mulletted gangly figure of our former singer, Chas. His captors had put him into a straight jacket and plonked a crash helmet onto his ginger head to stop him from hurting himself as he leapt around the stark empty space, shrieking like a mad thing. "Blimey, it really is him," I said to Jon. "I can hardly get my head round it."

"Yes, it's good to hear he hasn't lost his singing voice," Jon called over the manic shrieks of our former bandmate, "and such a stage presence too."

Chas was a great frontman for the band; the man knew no fear, probably enhanced by the repressed suburban upbringing he'd endured before the apocalypse.

We played the Students' Union a couple of times and he terrorised the crowd, jumping up on the bar and kicking drinks over, screaming into peoples' faces and pushing them around till they fled in terror. We'd start with a reasonable crowd, and by the end of the set there'd be a thin line of people cowering against the far wall.

This red-eyed maniac was now twice as scary as back then.

Having caught sight of his reflection in the mirror, Chas went for it like a terrier; his elongated teeth clacking against the glass. "Pity really," I said to Jon, "it would have been good to have got the band back together while we were in here. Looks like that won't be happening any time soon."

"On the contrary, good sir," Jon replied, pushing his glasses up his nose for dramatic effect like he was hosting an evening's gaming at Warhammer, "leave this to me. Decimated Population will ride again!"

That evening we met up for band practice in the bunker.

With the capable assistance of a couple of highly bribable orderlies, Jon smuggled Chas into the practice room and chained him to the wall. He left him in the straight jacket and, with proficient use of gaffer tape, he attached a microphone to the motorcycle helmet which he placed just in front of Chas's snarling mouth.

Chas totally went for me when I entered the room, but the chain held him back far enough for me to reach my guitar. Let's face it; it was not the first time in our acquaintance that I'd seen him reach the very end of his tether during band rehearsal. His head was jerking around and his exposed teeth chomped away in the direction of my cowering self as I nervously tuned-up.

"How good is this?" Jon asked, beaming at me from behind his kit. "Impressed?"

"Just like old times," I replied. "All we need is the Buckfast."

"Then behold," he said, "the pièce de resistance. If you would care to switch on the amplifier over there, you are in for a fucking big treat."

As I powered-up the amp, the room filled with an inhuman howling from Chas. Jon had added a slight echo to his voice - it sounded incredible. Like a banshee. Reverberating off the walls. Really fearsome. Picking up my guitar, I added the metal riff we had recently rehearsed and Jon added some blastbeats.

We recorded the session and played it back later while we enjoyed a beer in Security Guard Claire's cabin. There was one bit when Chas was thrashing his head back and forth between me and Jon, trying to get at us both, while howling like a mad dog.

Jon's team have been slow to develop the vaccine that will save us from the plague outside. And it looks like we're holed-up in the BUMHOLE Centre for quite a while. But we're not short of supplies, and between Security Guard Claire's small brewing operation and Plumber Dave's cannabis farm hidden out by the perimeter, we've had quite a party so far. Jon has kept Chas safe in the practice room and away from the laboratory. I don't know about you, but for me that's exactly what a true mate should do.

And both Jon and myself agree that our sessions down there in the bunker are by a long way the best music that any of us has ever made. I can just listen to those recordings over and over again.

Raging, killer tunes.

And Chas's vocal is totally infectious.

MakiNG PlaNS fOr NigeL

In which a group of friends plot their revenge on a small-minded oppressive bore, which may or may not involve getting the band back together. But it probably does.

Fuck me, that first glass of wine went down quickly. It didn't even touch the sides. As I walked into the party, there was a man stood in the foyer all done up with a nice white shirt, black waistcoat and a bow tie holding a silver tray of drinks - I could have kissed him. He didn't flinch when I put the empty glass back on the tray and took another. But all the trouble I had getting there I didn't feel any shame in bolting the first glass down - I had earned it.

Yeah, I was going to take the second at a slower pace, because it had been so long since I'd had a night off and there were a few hours ahead.

But I had some catching-up to do.

A lot of catching-up to do.

And a whole night without worry and responsibility.

Freedom.

I was going to get shit-faced.

Lucy had hired an All Bar One for her 40th. Not a place I would have chosen. Nor would she in her early days. But she'd gone all posh, or she thought she had. And I would have gone anywhere for a night off - I was really grateful for the invite.

We hadn't seen one another in about 18 months, but we kept in touch over Facebook and sometimes she'd post old photos of us, which were hilarious. Hair dyed all colours, home-made clothes and crazy make-up. Beaming at the camera from festivals, demos, gigs and nightclubs. Young and pretty and full of freedom.

Nigel didn't approve of course. He didn't approve of anything from my past. Lucy was OK for him, her job in PR, her husband Aleister who was some kind of business consultant, and her two privately educated children impressed him. Most of my other friends from my younger years, he repeatedly told me, were total losers or drug-addled mentalists or no-hopers with anger management issues.

I got a hard time from him if I met up with any of them. He'd stay grumpy for days. You know; the long silences, barbed comments, monosyllabic answers. In the end it wasn't worth it.

The things I'd had to put up with.

I got to the party late, which for me wasn't unusual. Nigel was playing up almost as much as the kids. He was accusing me of deleting his CV from the hard drive and I had to find it for him. Who doesn't back-up their CV for goodness sake? And it was for some stupid job he's going for, when he's only been in this one for two minutes. I don't think it was even about the CV, it was the thought of me having a night off that he didn't like. Or me having any friends at all, even the few he approved of. So I had to deal with that, and finding the kids' shoes and sort a meltdown (kids, not Nigel), while trying to cook them all dinner before I left the house. I didn't even have time to get ready properly - I looked a mess. But Lucy and her friends would just have to understand. I suppose most of them had gone through it all themselves. Oh yeah, then the train took ages to arrive because they only put on a restricted service after 6pm, and when it did come it was full of pissheads, and I had to sit in this carriage with all these loud, leery people, mostly blokes, without a drink, and I couldn't do my make-up in the toilet because it was so disgusting, and these yobs tried to get me to sit next to them, going, "Hey love, don't sit by yourself, come and join us." And the train stopped for 10 minutes just outside the station for no reason while all this mayhem with all these shouty blokes and screechy women went on around me. And town was full of dickheads - there must have been a match on or something - and the police were arresting someone at the station, and I'd got the wrong All Bar One because they've opened up a new one, and I tried to ask for directions but nobody knew where the new one was, so it took ages to find

the place, and the weather was completely shit so my hair
looked even more of a mess than when I left the house, so yeah,
I needed a fucking glass of wine when I got there. Is that
alright? Is that a problem?

I could hear some chatter in the main bar, but by the sound
of it, the party wasn't yet in full swing and I wasn't the last
to arrive. I must have looked awful, and I thought of turning
round and leaving.

What did I have in common with Lucy's friends anyway? They'd
think I was a right bore. All I did was look after kids and put
up with Nigel day after day, what would I have to talk about?
I couldn't remember the last time I'd been to a gallery or the
theatre. I couldn't even remember the last book I'd read all the
way through. And I bet Lucy's new, well-to-do friends got their
nannies to look after their children while they went and
sailed across the Atlantic, or trekked across South America,
or wrote their first novel, or ran a charity to dig wells for
deprived communities in Africa, or set up their own business
selling fucking cupcakes or something. And then put it all on
their blog. I wish I had the time.

But it had been such a struggle to get there that I gritted my
teeth and pushed through the swing doors into the bar. I could
feel the first flush of alcohol in my face, and I had a second
glass of wine in my hand for confidence. What's the worst that
could happen? I'd get drunk, make a fool of myself and have to
get a taxi home. Better than facing a Saturday night sat in
with Nigel in one of his moods.

Inside, there were a few groups of well-to-do women chatting
together, none of whom I knew. Seeing their lovely smart
clothes made me feel even more like the creature from the
black lagoon. With their nice hair and make-up, I bet they
didn't have to put up with the shit I had to deal with before
they left their houses tonight. I couldn't see Lucy anywhere,
even though it was her party, and to feel less uncomfortable
I perched on a stool by the bar to see if I recognised anyone.
If I didn't, I reasoned, I could just get myself another glass of
wine and drink myself onto the floor. People would expect that
kind of behaviour of someone who looked like a tramp who'd

come in off the street. Nothing unusual, nothing to see, move along now.

And then, approaching me across the All Bar One's wooden floor, I saw Beth. I froze and stared. She looked so ... shiny. That was the word, shiny. Shining with health, and confidence, and defiance, and joy. She looked like she did in the old photographs. Her face had a few lines, and her body had aged, but the same flame of life burned inside her now as it did back then. She stuck out a mile from the other women, just by what she was wearing - a long, bright purple pullover that stretched down beneath her hips, a short black skirt and black leggings with ankle-length purple Doc Martens. Not that she was scruffy, but her appearance was so different to the other women in the room. Her hair, although kept short, was wild, and her face without make-up shone with health. I could see her jet-black eyes twinkle in the lights of the bar and her white teeth flashed a broad smile.

Beside Beth was a teenage girl, I guessed was her daughter. She had her mother's defiant look, standing tall with her strong shoulders pulled back and looking the world in the eye. The sides of her head were shaved, and she'd pulled her long hair back in a pony tail.

I dreaded to think how many years it had been since I'd seen Beth. Since we'd played in bands together in our early twenties. Although we hadn't spoken in all that time, I had thought about her often. She was the one who put the energy and enthusiasm into what we did, the one who pushed things forward. She taught me to play the drums, and Lucy to play the bass. She wrote songs, booked gigs and even put our record out. We lost touch when Lucy went off to have kids. Beth moved down south to live in a squat in Birmingham or Bristol, I can't remember where. Somewhere beginning with B. Bath?

I thought of her the other week when I saw the homeless girl outside the bank. I was having one of my usual days running round like a blue-arsed fly, trying to transfer some money into our account so we didn't go overdrawn and get charged. It's like nothing could go right that day. For some reason I got locked out of the account so I couldn't get into it online,

43

and then the woman on the phone said I would need to go to
the bank in person and take some identification such as a
passport. I tried to explain to her that I had the kids to
look after and I couldn't just drop everything, but she said
that's the best they could do. And of course, they've closed the
branch that was nearest to us, so I had to herd the kids onto
the bus and go into town. And one of them had an accident on
the bus of course. Then there was a massive queue in the bank
because they only had one person behind the counter, despite
three other assistants milling about, but they were trying to
sell insurance or mortgages or something instead of helping
the customers. The kids were bored and started playing up - I
could totally understand what they were going through, but I
just had to get this thing sorted and I couldn't do anything
about it. When I did get to the front, the assistant had to go
to talk to her manager about it and I had to explain it all
over again until we got it all done. And when we finally got
outside, one of the kids had a meltdown in the street. She was
screaming her lungs out and in floods of tears while all these
office workers on their lunch breaks were walking past and
looking down their noses at us. But there's nothing you can do
- you've just got to be patient with them until they've calmed
down. While all this was going on, this girl came up to us and
asked me if I had any spare change. I was so distracted that I
couldn't do anything about it. She asked me again, and told me
she was homeless and was getting some money together for a
hostel that night. She was wearing a dirty anorak, and I could
see what must have been a grimy blue hoody underneath. But
it was her face that I remembered. She looked too young; too
innocent to be sleeping on the streets. She had big, wide, blue
eyes like a bushbaby, and a flush of red in her cheeks - from
youth, or alcohol, or both. I wanted to help her, but I'd had
such a frantic morning and with a screaming kid to deal with,
so I said, "Sorry, no."

Afterwards, the scene played through in my mind. That young
girl could have been one of us when we were her age. Any one
of us could have fallen onto hard times and ended up on the
street, especially with this Universal Credit and Bedroom
Tax they've foisted upon us. Goodness knows, a lot of us had
nearly been there. I thought about Beth; she was the wildest
of us. What had happened to her after she moved away? Could

something have happened that forced her onto the streets? Drugs? Debt? Bad relationship? It doesn't take much - life is so perilous when you think about it. And she lived so care-free, so precariously that it wouldn't have taken much to tip her over the edge. I wished I'd had the time to talk to that girl, to listen to her problems and to do something to help her. I still feel bad about it now. And I felt bad for not knowing where Beth was and that she was alright. But how much of this stuff can you carry around with you?

"Hey!" Beth had seen me and was bounding the remaining distance between us. She grabbed me in her arms and twirled me around the room. "I can't believe it," She beamed into my face; hers full of excitement and love. "Is it really you?"

I was overcome that she'd seen me, and even that she recognised me. After all this time. "I didn't know you were coming," I stammered. "What a lovely surprise. I hope I haven't spilled wine on you."

"Come on, let's get a bottle in," she said, "we've got so much catching up to do." Beth put her arm around my shoulders and walked me over to her daughter. "This is Molly," she said, "and here, Molly, is a very old friend I've been telling you about. She was even the drummer in my old band."

The girl smiled her mother's smile and said simply, "Cool."

"Molly is looking after me tonight in case I get a bit tipsy, aren't you Molly?" Beth said, hugging her daughter.

"I don't think you need looking after mum," she replied.

"You got any kids of your own?" Beth asked.

"A girl and a boy," I replied. "Three and five."

"Wonderful," Beth said. "You brought them with you?"

"No, I think they're both a bit too young to stay out this late. And they might wreck the place. You know what they're like at that age."

"Shame," Beth said, "I want to hear all about them. And I want to hear what you've been up to all these years. Come on, let's grab ourselves a table; we've got so much to talk about."

"Mum's told me all about you," Molly said. "The band sounds really cool." Molly looked 16 or 17, but she spoke to me like an equal. Like a friend.

"I'm surprised she even remembered," I replied, "it's so long ago now."

"Isn't it?" Beth said as she returned with a wine bottle and a couple of glasses. "Now tell me, are you still with your children's father? Sorry, but you don't like to assume these things."

"Him," I said. "Yes, we're still together, although sometimes I wonder why."

"Do I know him?" Beth asked.

"I don't think so," I replied. "He's called Nigel. He came along after you had left. He kind of hung around with us for a while. He wasn't into the same scene as we were. Don't get me wrong, he was OK - I did marry him after all. But let's talk about you - I've been thinking about you a lot over the years. What happened to you?"

"I've been thinking a lot about you too," Beth said. "Wondering where you were and hoping you were all right."

And so she told me about how she went to live on a commune after we lost touch; that there was no phone, let alone internet back then, which had made it easy for us to drift apart. She had Molly while she lived there and her little girl had grown up surrounded by all these people to look after her. Beth home-schooled Molly, and when she was still quite young they went travelling together across Spain and North Africa. They were more settled now, and Molly was due to start college in September - she wanted to be a filmmaker. All the time, I hung on her every word, enchanted by her rich, deep voice.

By the time she had finished, we were well into our second bottle and I was very light-headed. "So," Beth said, "now it's your turn. Tell me about your life."

I sat there like a rabbit caught in the headlights. I just stared into Beth's beautiful dark eyes for a moment. And then I saw my own face reflected in them. It was like staring at the still surfaces of two dark, deep pools. And I saw myself for what I was - tired, middle-aged, unkempt, unfulfilled, and too busy, too distracted, too worn out to do anything about it. Staring into Beth's eyes, I realised I wasn't coping - that life was slipping me by and I wasn't in control of my destiny, that I wasn't the adventurous, creative person I'd been all that time ago when Beth and I played in a band together. I'd lost that flame, or it had been taken from me; snuffed-out by life. Staring into Beth's eyes, I saw myself for what I was, and I cried. I fell forwards onto the table in floods of tears.

"Oh, come here honey," Beth said as she wrapped me in her arms. My shoulders quaked as she held me, and I heard Lucy's voice for the first time that night: "Is she alright?" She too threw her arms around me. I sat there in uncontrollable sobs, held in the arms of two of my oldest friends, while my tears spilled onto the table. But I was enclosed in the warmth of their friendship, protected from the world outside by kinship and love.

"I'm sorry," I said during a break in my tears.

"No, not your fault," Lucy assured me. "You do what you have to, you're with us now."

"It's just," I stammered, "it's just shit."

Lucy asked: "That fucking prick again? Just wait till I get my hands on him."

I told her it wasn't Nigel's fault; that I had been stuck in a life that I didn't want and I couldn't imagine a way out. That this was the first time I'd had a moment to relax since I couldn't remember when, and I'd lost the ability to think straight about anything a long time ago.

"Well I'm coming over to tell you both not to hurry," Lucy said. Just like Lucy, she and Aleister knew the owner, who'd agreed to keep the bar open late for us. "Let's get a brandy each," she added, "and to hell with life getting us down. Aleister, would you fetch us some drinks?"

"I'm sorry everybody," I said, "I'll be alright. I think the wine got to me."

"Nonsense," Beth said, looking to Lucy. "Sounds like we have a few things to sort out."

"Oh, I wish," I replied.

Aleister came over carrying the drinks in his two great hands. He made an imposing figure, dressed entirely in black with a black polo neck shirt under his jacket and a silver pentagram hanging around his neck. I remember his beautiful, transfixing jade-green eyes. "Ladies," he purred while lifting his glass, "it's good to see you back together again, and I would like to propose a toast. To undying friendship."

We laughed and clinked our glasses together. " Undying friendship."

Much later, when Lucy's friends had caught taxis home, there were just Beth, Molly, Lucy, Aleister and myself left around the table. We had spent the last couple of hours putting the world to rights, and my mood had lifted altogether. We reminisced loads, and the bar manager had been very patient with us while we shrieked with laughter. Three wild women together again. Lucy turned to me and said, "Hey, we have a confession to make."

"I'm sure you have," I laughed, "go on."

"It isn't by chance that we've ended up here together tonight. For a while now we've kept and eye on you and it seems to me that you're not happy with where life's been going."

"Well, you're not wrong," I said. "Don't misunderstand me, despite what I've said about him, Nigel's heart is in the right place.

But he doesn't do a damn thing to help and he's got this bee in his bonnet that he's providing for us all, when it's me who does everything. No wonder I'm always so exhausted."

"That man is dirt," said Beth.

"Well, if you put it like that," I said, "yes he is."

"So," said Beth, leaning towards me, her dark eyes twinkling in the candlelight, "we have to sweep away the dirt."

"Yes, that's all very well," I agreed, "but how? I can't move out because I've got nowhere to go and I've got the kids to think about. And we have a cat too - he's not going to look after it if he's left there on his own."

"That's just it," Lucy said, "we've got a little community here that we would like you to join. Now that Beth and Molly have taken hold of their senses and are moving up here, we think it would be the right time for you to come along too."

"Nigel would just love that," I laughed. "He doesn't even like me going to gigs, let alone joining a commune."

"Well, we've got just the thing for him," Beth said, reaching for the small rucksack she'd brought out with her. "This!" And out she pulled a crudely-made voodoo doll which she waved around the table. "So, I require three things from you; a photo of Nigel, something that's been close to him and a lock of his hair. And then we'll sort this Nigel out, for once and for all."

"Are we weaving witchcraft on him?" I laughed.

"Well, it can't make him any worse," said Lucy, laughing back at me. "You could say we're making plans for Nigel."

I rummaged through my bag and found a ticket for the dry cleaners - he'd asked me to pick his suit up the other day. Another job I forgot to do. I also gave Beth the picture Nigel had given me; the one of him on one of his fishing expeditions, looking all pleased with himself and holding up an enormous carp that he'd caught. I don't know why I'd carried it around - it was such a ridiculous image. I always felt sorry for the fish; pulled from the cool, deep waters and left to flounder on the riverbank while Nigel paraded his inflated ego at its expense. I felt an affinity with it, slowly suffocating at the hands of this stupid, self-absorbed man. Its helplessness reminded me of my own situation.

"I also have a confession to make," Lucy said to me. "I kind of knew this would happen sometime, and when that prick last deigned to invite me over your threshold, I had a look in your bathroom and pulled out a lock of his hair from the plughole of the shower." She held up a small clear bag which contained a ball of his unmistakeable, unremarkable dull brown hair.

"Well, girls, let's have some fun," said Beth as she produced a length of black twine and wrapped the ticket, photo and tuft of hair around the Nigel doll. "You first." She handed me a long silver pin which had a small, jet black ball at one end and a devilishly sharp point at the other.

"You want me to stick the pin into Nigel?" I asked. To which the whole table roared "Yes!"

"Well," I said, "he can be a real pain in the neck, so that's where the pin is going. See how you like it Nigel." My friends cheered as I jabbed the pin into Nigel's neck, and I must say, I hadn't felt that good in ages; so unburdened, and so empowered. I felt like I could fly.

"Me now," said Beth taking the doll from me and a pin from Lucy. "I've got a headache just hearing about him, so I'm going to stick it here." And she rammed home the pin into the Nigel doll's head to more cheers from the table. "Now you Lucy."

Lucy laughed recklessly while she wielded the third pin menacingly at Nigel. "With joy," she said. "Well, I always thought he was a right pain in the..." She gripped Nigel tightly in her fist and poised to strike the pin. "I always thought he was a right pain in the ... in the arse." And, to screams of merriment from the rest of us, she rammed the pin into Nigel's jacksie, right up to the black ball at the end, which protruded like a little rabbit's tail.

"More drinks," Lucy called above the furore.

"Hang on," I shouted, "I've got another one I want to do.
Aleister, what's that pint you're drinking?"

"It's a traditional pint of bitter," he replied. "Pendle Witch.
Quite appropriately."

"Yes, how appropriate Aleister," I shrieked, now filled with
drink and adrenalin. "Well, if you will excuse me Aleister,
but I always thought that Nigel should drown in his own
bitterness." And I plunged the doll head first into Aleister's
drink, so that the legs and the black bauble stuck out of the
top. We roared with laughter, as Damienne the bar manager
mysteriously appeared at the table with another tray of
drinks.

Do I need to say I didn't make it home that night? Well, I
didn't. Nigel hasn't really spoken to me since, but I count
that as a good thing. I woke up on Lucy's sofa with a blinding
hangover. There was a half-finished glass of Blossom Hill on
the coffee table next to me, and I never drink that. After the
bar, we all came back to Lucy's and listened to records into
the early hours. One thing for Lucy, she always had an amazing
record collection. We dug out stuff I hadn't heard in years
- Bikini Kill, Slits, X-Ray Spex, Xmal Deutchland, even some
bands I didn't know - gothy post-punk from Spain, all-female
US hardcore bands and weird experimental Japanese stuff. Some
time into this session, we agreed it would be a good idea to
get the band back together, although I don't know if the others
will remember that. It would be fun though.

So when I rolled in after midday, Nigel just grunted at me and
said he expected me to have stayed out with "those women". That
was it. In the afternoon, I killed a couple of hours taking the
kids to the park, to get away from him as much as anything.
It was great though. The kids loved it - the sun was out for
the first day of May, and they ran around on the grass and
we played on the swings. The beautiful fresh air cleared my
hangover too and we stayed out as long as we could. After that,
me and the kids had a film night together, while Nigel sat in
the back room, which he calls his "study", doing whatever he

does on the internet. I never bothered to ask what it was, and I had stopped caring by that time. I must have fallen asleep on the sofa because I heard him leave in the morning. He had his fishing basket with him, so I guessed he would be out all day. He didn't bother to say goodbye, even to the kids.

I made my mind up. I texted Lucy: "I'll take you up on your offer if still open." Life has many chapters; that's one thing I learned the previous evening when I met up with Beth and Lucy. And this felt like the beginning of a new chapter for me.

Moments later, my phone went. "Coming right over," Lucy replied. "Stay where you are."

I spent the next hour getting the kids ready, just packing the essentials while the cat sat by the door watching us patiently. Alicat wasn't even fazed when the kids wanted to play with her. She just sat and watched; her eyes jade-green, like Lucy's partner Aleister's, against her jet black fur. It's as if she had been watching over us, quietly and patiently, all along.

And now she was waiting for the door to open, as if she was waiting for the next chapter to begin.

Chew ON ThiS

In which a band member is chewed-up and spat out by the machinations of the music industry, only to find salvation from an unexpected source, and salivation with an unexpected sauce.

...Thanks for asking. Yes, I'm looking forward to the reunion, and the tour looks interesting, so it's going to be fun going back on the road. How's that? More?

OK, what can I say? I'm well on with the album as we planned all those years ago. In fact, it's not so much a reunion, but the next phase of the original business outline. Without its creators. Obviously. No coming back for those two.

Sorry, would you like to eat first, or shall we plough on through the interview and get something afterwards? I'm happy if you are. Well, our story begins with Neil and Paul, who sketched out the plan when they were at Nottingham Trent business school. It went along the lines of: a pretty standard indie release; major label; three albums; split; reunion; and all the merch, best-of albums, live albums and so on in between.

It doesn't sound revolutionary now, but at the time they were really ahead of their game. If you went to business school, you were expected to be a square - their genius was convincing people they were cool. And that was some feat at Nottingham Trent. Having constructed their business plan, they recruited me to write the music. I went to music school in Bath Spa by the way and was actually once a finalist in Young Jazz Musician of the Year. They stuck me on bass out of the way.

I didn't know much about that kind of ska-punk they had in mind when they first approached me, but they gave me a big stack of CDs and asked me to write an album. It was basic stuff, but catchy and gave me room to have fun with brass arrangements. I played most of the music for the first album Chew on This and the EP, Inedibles' Flavoured Calories, myself.

The titles weren't mine - they came from some marketing survey Neil and Paul conducted, something to do with our target audience of impressionable suburban teenagers and related to our merchandise. In fact, I'm sure they pinched "Flavoured Calories" from a sci-fi novel. Good title though.

Neil and Paul had me working on Completely Inedible straight away to avoid what they called a "difficult second album" - you know, the one where a band pours its ideas into its first album and then struggles to find the same inspiration and energy for the follow-up.

For me, Completely Inedible suffered from over-production, but it had a long time to market and they played around with it for a whole a year between meetings with record labels and lawyers, while they dotted the i's and crossed the t's.

Otherwise, they got on with the branding and marketing while I played around with some more tunes. The money hadn't started to come in by that time, but it was an easy life. It was all highlighted on the business plan's timeline which predicted high sales during the reunion phase; that's one reason why I'm now looking forward to going back on the road.

Anna's vocal carried Chew on This - she made that album something special. And she came a long way in a short time too. You can hear a few of her original recordings on the retrospective album, The Inedibles' Sell By...

Again, the business plan required a female singer. Neil and Paul initially reckoned male singers sell better (completely ignoring jazz artists), but their market research into gender breakdown showed a large, independent, reasonably wealthy and mostly ignored population of young women who would identify with a female singer. "We need something unique that will propel the strategy," they told me.

Anna was Romanian by birth and had these really piercing dark eyes. She was 16 when she auditioned, and it must have been hard for her to join an established group of three older males. Well, Neil and Paul generally left me by myself with the music, but you know what I mean. I can see why she felt the odd one out.

She didn't possess the range or technical ability of the singers I'd previously backed, but she made up for that with an eerie ferocity - I'd never encountered a stage presence like hers. She was quite scary in real life too, but I guess we bonded while talking about the music while Neil and Paul looked after the business end of things.

Well, Neil and Paul set up a deal with an indie label called Year's Supply to co-release Chew on This and Flavoured Calories, which involved some chicanery with publishing rights or something. The label called the plan, "An excellent road map for future growth." I didn't understand what the label's role was, but it got us to where they could negotiate the deal with the major label, Worker/Consumer, while I twiddled around with Completely and got some ideas together for the third long-player, The Inedible Beige Album.

OK, the title wasn't great, but the cover more than made up for it. The artwork came from a photo of the buffet at Neil's wedding - a traditional spread of sausage rolls, pork pies, ham sandwiches vol-au-vents - all beige and meat-based. The irony did not go unnoticed that this was totally inedible for vegetarians like myself, Anna and a few of the other musicians he'd invited.

Neil programmed his wedding as neatly as he had the band's first break-up. I'd long anticipated the date from the spreadsheet they showed me, and had plenty of time to plan ahead. They'd scheduled it half-way through the release-tour cycle, citing fatigue and musical differences, and they wanted it to shock our fans, which would tee us up for the retrospective releases and the reunion. Neil and Paul had some non-musical projects lined up, and I wanted to get back to playing real music again. Anyway, after the first two albums, it was all beginning to feel like a regular job.

Neil and Paul cleverly fulfilled the major label's three-album deal with a live recording, (Inedibly Yorkshire), which saved me having to write another one. They'd also lined-up the best-of (Inedibles' Sell by...) and even a tribute (The Inedibles Regurgitated). This is all common practice in today's industry, but back then, when you split you split for good, leaving

adoring fans to either weep for evermore over fading posters
of their favourite pop stars, or move on to whatever band next
caught their eye.

The reunion album was planned to be called Inedibles
Defrosted, and Neil and Paul would contact me in advance so we
could implement the next phase of the plan. Meanwhile, they
said, the royalties from Sell by... and Regurgitated would keep
us all in clover.

Although Neil and Paul took care of the business, legal,
publishing and marketing sides of The Inedibles, I considered
myself to belong to their inner circle - after all, I was privy
to the business plan. I had told them that it was unfair to
freeze Anna out of the plan, especially as she had so admirably
filled the role of fronting The Inedibles, and they promised to
inform her of the wider scheme as soon as was practicable.

But what they did was a shock even to me.

I knew we'd announce it to the music press halfway through
the Inedible Beige Album tour; we'd play one more show and
cancel the other gigs. So when I was mobbed by journalists,
well if three journalists constitutes a mob, in the hotel lobby
after the Birmingham show, I had my lines well-rehearsed:
"Musical differences. Tour fatigue. No further comment. Record
label will release a detailed statement in due course."

Seeing Neil and Paul hadn't made it down for breakfast that
morning, I assumed this was in their business narrative and
they were keeping a low profile. But I did think it unusual
that none of the crew were down there either. I got myself
some dry toast and black coffee, which was standard tour
fare for me back then - Neil and Paul said it would be too
expensive to cater for vegetarians and other fussy eaters.

When Anna walked in, she was in bits. She'd been collared
by one of the hacks in the lobby and of course she'd known
nothing about the split. Plus the journalists gave her a
harder time than they'd given me. After all, I was only the bass
player; the songs weren't even in my name - they were credited
simply to "The Inedibles Music Publishing Ltd". She was crying

and her mascara had run down her ashen face.

Until then, I hadn't appreciated that the split would have affected her so much. I guess I was swept along by Neil and Paul with their business plan. For myself, I had very little emotional investment in the band, and at the back of my mind I would return to playing the music I loved.

As it turned out, that wasn't to happen. When I eventually got over the split, I spent some years scratching a living as a music tutor.

Well, I tried my best to placate Anna and I told her as much as I could - that it wasn't as bad as it sounded and once Neil and Paul had talked her through their business plan, she'd see the bigger picture. Anna fixed her fierce eyes on me. "Those smarmy public school bastards," she screamed over the hubbub of the hotel breakfast room, "what have you let them do to us?"

I began to explain that it was all part of their business vision and that we would be free to pursue other projects - possibly a solo career for herself - while the royalties came pouring in. But she turned her back on me mid-sentence and stormed out of the hotel, stopping briefly, I heard a short while later, to punch one of the journalists and break his nose.

Well the next year or two are still a blur. Firstly, I was to learn that the whole crew, including Neil and Paul, had checked out early that morning, and I was never to speak to them again. Just like that. Then I was flat broke - Neil and Paul looked after the books and gave me what they called a "per diem" payment out of our advance to cover daily costs while we were on tour.

I remember hitch-hiking from somewhere along Coventry Road, which took an age. And when I got back to London, all hell broke loose. Sorry, this part is still difficult to talk about.

Well, the record label wouldn't take my calls, and refused to see me, even when I sat in the lobby. Then I started to get all these legal letters saying I owed money to all sorts of people.

I got some assistance from the Citizens' Advice Bureau, and it turned out that whatever paperwork I'd signed way back when the three of us had first sat down together only entitled me to an income as a session musician.

It also transpired that the company we'd set up to handle The Inedibles' affairs, Inedible Assets Ltd, went into liquidation and Neil and Paul had removed their names as directors and as persons with significant control, leaving yours truly as the sole director. Again, I had signed documents which I didn't understand.

And all the while, from what we could work out, the record company advance, minus royalties recouped out of the said advance, and plus anything we'd started to make as a band, had been drip-fed to other companies, some of which were registered overseas. I remember one was in Luxembourg. And another in Bermuda. It was such a tangle, I didn't have a hope of establishing what had actually gone on. Plus, as I said before, I was broke - Neil and Paul paid for my flat and gave me expenses while I wrote the music, and I stupidly assumed that the three of us were equal partners. Bandmates. I couldn't afford a proper solicitor - I had to work it all out myself.

I was devastated. It took ages to convince everyone that I hadn't been responsible for the band's finances, and that I couldn't pay the bills, even though I wished I could. The woman from the Citizens' Advice recommended I declare myself bankrupt, and I moved back in with my mum. Then I had some kind of weird breakdown, which put me out of action for a long time.

It was my counsellor who suggested I take up music again. During our sessions, we worked it through that I equated playing music with my experiences in The Inedibles. So I stopped playing any instrument at all. Tentatively, on her suggestion, I picked up the sax and worked through the scales for an hour or two a day. It felt good and gave me the headspace I needed to pull things round again. Within a year, I had begun to tutor young musicians, and that has been my income ever since.

But when I thought things had settled down again, life threw me another curveball, when a student's mum recognised me as a former member of The Inedibles.

I was lucky that I was so anonymous in the band that I could get on with my life without people recognising me and wanting to talk to me about those days. Occasionally, I'd get a sideways look from an ageing skapunk, but mostly I was left alone.

But then, when one of my students' parents dropped off her daughter for her weekly clarinet lesson, she asked me if we knew one another from somewhere else. I told her that I was sure we didn't and left it at that. The following week, she told me she recognised me as the guitarist of The Inedibles, and confided that she had been a big fan in her younger days. After I corrected her that I played bass guitar in the band, and that I wasn't in touch with the music business any longer, she asked me what had happened to Anna. "She was such a massive influence on me," she confessed. "I want my daughter to be just like her."

I hadn't stopped to think of Anna since she left the hotel that morning. I didn't have a family contact for her, and let's face it, I was so utterly destroyed by the situation with Neil and Paul that I had blocked all thoughts of The Inedibles completely from my mind.

"Well," I said, trying to get rid of my student's mum, "it's good that people remember us."

"Many do," she replied. "And more come." She stared at me long and hard and extended her hand for me to shake. I noticed a small tattoo on her palm; a circled A.

A short while later I received a phone-call from the mother of a prospective pupil to enquire whether I could tutor her daughter in the cor anglais. I told her it was an instrument of which I had little knowledge (outside of its use my mum's favourite soap opera, Emmerdale), but I advised that I could assist her daughter with theory. "Capital idea," she said, and we booked a lesson for the following week.

Her daughter Elizabeth was a strange-looking child; taller than most of her age with unkempt flame-red hair and piercing dark eyes. But it turned out that she was proficient on the cor anglais. I asked her to play something to assess her level, and she had given a full half hour of haunting, mournful melodies before I emerged from the deep, reflective mood into which I had gently sunk before we had the chance to talk.

I asked her how she had become so skilful on the instrument and who her previous tutor had been. "My mother," she replied directly.

"I haven't seen either of you in Carshalton before," I said. "Are you new to the area? South Croydon perhaps? Or Purley?"

"More," Elizabeth replied, "come." And she opened the palm of her raised hand to display the same tattoo - a circled A - that I had seen on the parent who had enquired after Anna a few weeks previously.

"I'm sorry," I stammered, unsettled by the child's behaviour. "I don't understand."

"Morecambe," she said. "We're from Morecambe."

"What brings you to our neck of the woods?" I asked.

"We're here for you," she replied. "It is time. Anna would like you both to become reacquainted once more. She has summoned you to Morecambe."

My mind reeled at the sound of Anna's name. Until recently, I gladly had almost forgotten the terrible episode of The Inedibles. But here I was in the parlour of my mother's home, summoned to a seaside resort way up in the north-west of England by a peculiar-looking child and her haunting music, whose dark eyes shone at me like two fragments of jet.

The trepidation I felt on the long haul up the country was tempered by thoughts of the debt that I owed to Anna for the way she had been treated all that time ago. As I stared

cubesville

from the window seat of the Pendelino's quiet coach, I assured
myself that this would finally put paid to that terrible
episode in Birmingham.

While we rattled through the Home Counties and the Midlands,
I contemplated the upset that the split must have caused to
one so young, and how difficult it would have been for her to
regain any trust in the people around her. I was, I concluded,
honoured that she would even talk to me again.

On my arrival, the magnificent view across Morecambe Bay more
than compensated for the standard of the accommodation I
had booked. Having dropped my bags at Neptune's Garden, I left
its proprietor to recover from what looked like a heavy, but
routine lunchtime session and I took a stroll along the wind-
lashed Promenade.

It was August and steel-grey clouds hung over the bay, fearsome
and thrilling. Brutalised by briny gusts, I was swept eastwards
in search of my rendez vous with The Inedibles' former singer.

Elizabeth Bathory, my curious scholar of the cor anglais, told
me to meet Anna at the old cinema on the Promenade at 3pm,
but I was damned if I could find the location. The nearest I
got was a shabby-looking multiplex beside a Kentucky Fried
Chicken outlet, which I knew was not Anna's style. My search
along the Promenade did, however, reveal an impressive art deco
hotel and plenty of second-hand shops in which to shelter.

Somehow, I ended up in a second-hand record shop somewhere
behind the Promenade. If Anna had maintained her musical
connections in such a small town, I reasoned, then perhaps she
would be known to the proprietor. On a whim, I leafed through
the punk and ska section of their 12" vinyl racks, hoping to
recognise some of the bands with whom we shared the bill all
that time ago.

And you can guess what I found.
There it was in all its splendour. The original 12" LP of The
Inedibles' Beige Album - the one we had been touring when we
split. The cover was near enough in mint condition, depicting
Neil's wedding buffet - for which he thoughtlessly provided

a meat-based spread without a care for his bandmates. Like we weren't important. Like we were cattle to be exploited, I thought, before he moved on.

And if discovering an actual record for which I had written the music, and on which I played all the instruments, hadn't sent my heart racing fast enough, the price brought from me a gasp of disbelief.

£17.50!

Can you imagine that! In the years I spent away from the music business, our record had almost doubled in value. £17.50! What, I wondered, would our indie label releases on Year's Supply fetch? Probably the better side of £25. I wished I'd kept hold of them, I thought - I'd be raking it in by now.

The teenage punk behind the counter eye-balled me like I was some nutter come in off the street to shelter from the terrible weather. I suppose I must have cut a strange figure leafing through the punk and ska section with the rain dripping from my scruffy orange cagoule. "Hallo," I called across the shop, while pulling back the hood of my jacket - the better to hear my interlocutor. "I wondered if you could help me with some directions."

"Sure thing," she replied. "You lost? Don't show them you're lost this end of Morecambe - bit rough round here sometimes."

"Really?" I asked, quite taken aback that an unassuming Victorian terrace could harbour any such delinquency. "I'm looking for the old cinema, the one on the Prom."

"Cinema? No cinema on the Prom I'm afraid, unless you mean the one just past the Aldi. There's the old Alhambra, but that's about to be turned into flats. Shame. Developers - just a bunch of greedy bastards, aren't they?"

"Yes," I agreed, not sure what I was agreeing to. "Shame. Well, I'll carry on looking." And then as an after-thought I asked about the album: "Is this a collector's item? £17.50 sounds a lot of money."

"Someone will want it," she replied. "We get people from all over the place - some from as far as Preston - coming in here looking for the old stuff. And more come."

"I'm excited to hear that," I said, "because you see ... I played in this band. Here, look..." I opened up the gatefold sleeve to where I remembered there was a photograph of the four of us.

And there I was, blurred and out of focus, standing behind Neil and Paul, who in turn stood behind the resplendent, indomitable, Anna.

Holding that record after so many years, I sadly reflected that I hadn't received a credit on the album - something to do with a mistake at the printers, Paul told me. He was furious about it at the time, and explained that he was prepared to recall every single album from the shops. But after some discussion, we agreed that it was probably best to amend the cover for the reissue and to make doubly sure there was no recurrence on the compilation he and Neil had planned for after the split.

"It's you!" the proprietor shouted. "You're the guy from The Inedibles! Sick! You should have said. I never expected that you were coming to the shop before your reunion with Anna. Well, you've made my day."

"You know Anna?" I asked. "And me? And The Inedibles?"

"Of course dude," she replied. And she opened up the palm of her hand to display the same circled-A tattoo that adorned the hands of my student's mum and young Elizabeth of cor anglais dexterity.

"You need to get going," she continued, "you're late as it is. You want the Alhambra - left on the Prom and on the corner of Lancashire Street." She ushered me out of the shop and back in the direction of the seafront. The whole episode in the record shop had left me stunned; finding The Inedibles' album, recognised as a member of the band, and not least the strange tattoo. "I'll be along later," the young punk called after me, "I wouldn't miss this for the world."

I had wandered past the Alhambra a few times that afternoon without recognising it as "the old cinema". This wasn't helped by a large fishing tackle shop, which stretched along several units to mask the picture house behind. But equipped with directions from the young punk in the record shop, I now found the cinema's entrance - a doorway on the street corner, beside which was a fading poster for a night of wrestling; a sorry token of the cinema's terminal decline. Another notice declared the beautiful old building's greatest indignity, it was to be developed into town centre apartments.

I pushed open the door and mounted the stairs, towards where I could hear amplified voices in the hall above. It sounded like a large meeting was in progress, with a live debate over a PA system. This, I assumed, would have something to do with Anna's invitation that I meet her here today.

"...become instantaneously dissociated from the thing they produce." Was that Anna's voice I could hear as I ascended the staircase? She sounded bolder, more assertive than I remembered, but still maintained a trace of her central European accent. "From my own experience, ownership alienates us from our own cultural output..."

A second voice: "I will have to interrupt you there. Yes. I can confirm the person we've all been waiting for has arrived. People, let's hear it for... Let's hear it for the bass player from The Inedibles."

As I entered the wide room to the applause of a full house, I forgave the compère for momentarily forgetting my name. The rush I got walking through that cheering crowd took me right back to playing with the band. I took to the stage like the intervening years hadn't happened and waved my gratitude to the audience.

And just like the old days, Anna had already taken centre stage. The years had hardly touched her. She may have combed-out the long dredds she wore when she fronted The Inedibles which, when she shook them, seemed to fill the stage, but her hair retained its midnight sheen and her moon-like complexion hardly showed a wrinkle.

"On behalf of everyone gathered this afternoon," she announced across the hall, "I would like to thank you for making the long journey up here today. We have come together in our home town of Morecambe to discuss the debasing aspects of capitalism and to debate the next steps forward. My friends, this person, my former bandmate, as much as anyone, fully appreciates what we have discussed this afternoon - a capitalist system that seeks only to devour."

She turned her piercing dark eyes towards me. "Thank you Anna," I said. "It's amazing to see you again. And yes, I agree totally with what you're saying. I was chewed up and spat out." I was relieved to hear murmurs of agreement from the audience.

"This artist knows what it's like to see their work, their dreams, commodified and consumed by the ambition of others. In their pursuit of wealth, did they not leave you jobless, homeless and hopelessly in debt? Were you not consigned to scratching a living by making the most basic use of your talents?"

Considering I'd ascended a flight of stairs off the street and stepped straight into a strange situation I didn't understand, I felt uncommonly at ease in Anna's presence, like we'd rolled back the years, that we were in The Inedibles together and this was a standard gig for us.

Turning to her I replied, "I'd never thought of it in that way, Anna, but if you put it like that, then yes. That's what they did to me - they hung me out to dry." A few shouts of outrage echoed round the hall - the crowd, it appeared, was ready to get on my side and whatever I had walked into, I thought, it was something I was probably going to enjoy. I hadn't been in front of an audience like this since that last gig in Birmingham and I looked into those faces with the same confidence as I did then. This is how it should have been all that time - Anna and me, and an appreciative crowd.

"And you watched powerless," she continued, "while they erased your name from history, leaving you without any rights over the songs you wrote?"

"Hell yes!" I shouted in response, which in turn met with raucous cheers from the crowd. "They left me with the debts," I yelled to yet more appreciative roars. "They stole my work and left me without a penny. What they lack in imagination and skill, they make up for in knowing how to steal from those who create. They're parasites." This last statement nearly brought the house down. All those wasted years spent just existing; living at mum's and teaching the children of well-meaning but boring suburban families the same tedious scales and the same tedious tunes; it all came out on that stage with Anna.

"More than parasites," Anna called over the noise from the crowd, "they're predators! Parasites rarely kill the host, yet these predators bled what they could from you and left you for dead. Like a sacrificial lamb on the cold, hard, granite altar of Mammon."

"Yes, Anna, that's it," I shouted in reply. "They're cannibals, nothing but cannibals."

The now hysterical crowd began to chant, "Cann-i-bals! Cann-i-bals!" over and over. Some pumped the air with their fists.

I always maintained that Anna had an unparalleled stage presence, and it was never truer than now. Anna raised her hands to quell a sustained period of chanting. "Listen up," she called, "for my bandmate knows the truth. Even this dried-out, defeated husk can see what caused our fate. We all know it - capitalism is cannibalism." Turning back towards me she asked, "What do you say? Capitalism is cannibalism?"

I took her cue and strode to the front of the stage, placed my right foot firmly on the monitor, threw my fist into the air and with all that was left of my husky voice screamed, "Capitalism is cannibalism!"
"Today we take the power back," Anna announced to the baying crowd. "As artists, as musicians, as workers; anyone who sees what they produce taken from them and monetised by others. Today is the day the people cannibalise capitalism! People ... comrades ... fellow outcasts ... eat the rich!"

Deafening roars of "Eat the rich" rocked the room that day.

"Bring them on." Our compare, who had waited patiently in the wings, again took to the stage. "People, on stage together for the last time, here they are, reunited for one final performance. Come on, make some noise and give it up for The Inedibles."

While the frenzied horde continued chanting, "Eat the rich! Eat the rich!", I stood dumbstruck. What on earth had I got myself into? How was this even happening? Were the two musicians who fled that Birmingham hotel all those years ago really going to join us on stage in Morecambe? Were we expected to perform a reunion gig here in this seafront picture house? Without a soundcheck? Where were our instruments? Who was going to set up the drum kit?

And then over the PA came our song, Hungry for More. Not one of my finest compositions I must say - Paul got me to write it as a crowd pleaser. To inspire me, we listened to some 1980s rock albums together round at his apartment one evening over a cheap bottle of Rioja. It didn't sit well in our set, but I accepted his business sense over my artistic judgement and went along with his decision.

This crowd went wild for it, all credit to him (which he, quite literally took). "I don't think I should," went his lyric, "and it does me no good, but I'm hungry for more, hungry for more." The words weren't to my liking, but Paul added them only after I recorded all the instruments myself. The crowd was totally loving it though, and their wild dancing resembled a Bacchanalian orgy. They seemed to particularly enjoy the chorus, "Hungry for more, hungry for more."

And then I saw them.

How could I have been so slow off the mark? I guess deep down, despite the frenzied spectacle of the audience going mad for our song, I still held the conservative values that had kept me chained to my life as a music tutor, living all this time in my mother's house in Carshalton. A life I hadn't chosen for myself, but which was all that remained after everything else had been taken from me, and which I had been afraid to relinquish. A yawning suburban tedium - a Tuesday afternoon

that stretched on for ever. An empty tree-lined avenue along
which the windows of each identical home was lit with the TV
glow from the same narrow choice of entertainment, and beyond
which nothing else existed.

Seeing Neil and Paul turned my world upside down. Although
what happened next has dimmed in my memory, I have not
returned to Carshalton, nor shall I again. How could I after
what I did that afternoon? And after what I witnessed others
doing?

Naked, bleeding and terrified, Neil and Paul were wheeled onto
the stage, each bound tightly to a pole and motionless; their
frightened eyes darted around the hall, desperately attempting
to comprehend the scene before them.

Despite his terrible predicament, I could see that the years
had been good to Neil, who was in fine shape for a man
of his age; having avoided the middle-aged spread of his
contemporaries and looking like he enjoyed an athletic life,
healthy diet and plenty of sunshine. Paul, if the girth of his
midriff and sag of his jowls were any measure, looked like he
enjoyed the high-life - good food, fine wine. Both in their own
ways enjoyed the trappings of the wealth they had accumulated
over all this time. Probably at the expense of other people -
how many more victims followed Anna and myself?

Anna's stagehands wheeled on two braziers of hot coals, and
positioned one in front of each panicked former bandmate. I
know it sounds strange, but seeing the two again gave me a
sense of comfort and closure. After Birmingham, it seemed like
I hadn't drawn breath to make sense of things. I'd just accepted
what little opportunity was left to me and stagnated. But
now I felt I could finally move on. I saw them for what they
were - exploiters of other people's creativity. People who, in
their accrual of wealth, took away the opportunity afforded to
others, limited their outlook. Even shortened their lives.

Until now I clung like a drowning sailor to the notion that
this was some bizarre spectacle constructed by Anna to terrify
Neil and Paul into apologising for their actions and making
some kind of repair. But with all the shouts of "Capitalism

is cannibalism", "Eat the rich", and the latest - reduced to a
simple, "Bar-be-cue", I understood that the fates of my former
bandmates were sealed.

Anna confirmed this last thought when she turned to me again
and asked bluntly and directly, "What do you say? Are we going
to eat the rich?"

Recognition flickered in Neil's eyes. "Oh God," he cried, "you're
the bass player in that band. You're errrm, the bass player.
The jazz player from Brighton. No, Bristol? You're the jazz
player." Whether it was fear, or that his memory of the time
we shared in The Inedibles had been lost in some void between
Birmingham and Morecambe, Neil struggled to remember my
name. "Look mate," he continued, "get us out of here. We'll make
it worth your while - we can do a deal. What do you say mate?
Do it for old times' sake. Just get us away from these psychos.
Hey, let's get a band together - it can be like back in the day.
Please, mate, get us out of here."

Maybe it was seeing Anna for the first time since Birmingham,
and maybe it was hearing my song, Hungry for More, for which
I received no royalties. Far from rewarding me with fame,
fortune or just the dignity we all deserve, the exploitation
of my creative output led to debt, mental illness and years
of tedium. I was left too depressed, too low, and too defeated
to drag myself out of it and to enjoy this beautiful world.
Whether Neil and Paul had consciously written it into The
Inedibles' business plan, I pondered, or whether I was mere
collateral damage in their campaign. They used my skills as a
musician without a thought of paying me and they used their
own legal and commercial talents to ensure I never would be
paid.

I looked at Neil, who was now pleading for mercy, and back to
Anna, whose strength radiated through the hall and livened
the spirit of each person there, empowering us to stand up to
life, and bestowing on us a collective strength and confidence
to take control and change it.

"Fuck yeah," I shouted. "Cannibal-anarchy!"

What followed was the greatest stage invasion I had ever
seen, even in the height of The Inedibles' popularity. I was
lifted onto the shoulders of hysterical, half-naked hedonists
while the shouts, the smoke and finally the barbecue smell
that emanated from the seething stage below spelled-out my
bandmates' fate.

"Let's see how inedible they really are," Anna called up, as she
handed me what looked like a sizeable chunk of Paul's buttock
between slices of poppy seed cob, dribbling with Dijon mustard
and ketchup. I shrieked with laughter and was lost in Anna's
dark eyes.

Considering it was the first meat I had eaten in many, many
years, I was somewhat relieved the next morning to find I
didn't have the bad guts and bad food hangover I anticipated,
when I awoke sandwiched between two equally naked fellow
revellers. While I stretched and admired the view out across
the bay, I saw that during the night I had obtained a tattoo
on the palm of my right hand. I hadn't a clue how it got there,
nor did I care. The circled A looked pretty cool, I thought. I
still have it now. Here.

"You're alive then." Anna, too, was admiring the view.
Yesterday's storm had passed and the azure sea lapped against
the snow-white boulders of the rock revetment flood defences,
which Morecambe Council had considerately placed to protect
this jewel in the north's coastal crown. She had watched over
me while I slept.

"Anna, did we really eat Neil and Paul?" I asked, as memories of
the previous night's debauchery came flooding back; the fatty
texture of Paul and almost unchewable gristle of Neil still
clinging to my palate like they couldn't let go.

"We feasted on the carcass of capitalism, if that's what you
mean," she replied. "It surprised me how many proletarian
mouths you can feed with just two capitalists. Redistributing
the corporeal manifestation of creative exploitation goes a
long way."

"Well, with the hours Neil spent in the gym, bulked out by

Paul's good living, we obtained plenty of calories from the capitalists," I said. And then with a pang of guilt added, "Anna, what have we done? What crimes did we commit?"

"What we've done," she replied, "is what they did to us. That morning in Birmingham, they took what they wanted from us and left us to our wits without a care if we lived or died. We were their cash cows, and they milked us dry and fed us to the flames. But it was they who received the final grilling."

"Anna, I feel so bad for what they did to you," I confessed. "I knew they had a plan, but I was a fool to think that they would treat us as equals - that we'd share everything together. Now I know that the rich don't like to share. Anything. I was so trusting, so stupid to go along with them. They cheated us Anna."

"I felt sorry for you when I saw what they were doing," she said. "I could see how they were using you and setting you up. But I was so young - my voice was stilled by the patriarchal nature of their business structure and I felt powerless to intervene. All these years, I've kept an eye out for you - I sent students down to your mother's in Carshalton to keep you in business and to report back to me that you were still alive, while I went after those two scoundrels."

Anna explained that after Neil and Paul left her marooned in Birmingham, she wandered from place to place, ending up in a bedsit in Morecambe. From here, she established a network of dispossessed people; seaside towns are full of them - forgotten people who live close to wealth but scramble for unrewarding seasonal work with nothing to do in the long, dull, depressing winters when half the town is boarded-up - too broke to participate in town life.

The tattooed A was Anna's idea - it was "Anna's-key" - a collective escape from the tedium most people experience under a capitalist system; escape, empowerment, enablement for the forgotten. Anarchy.

When the time was right, she explained, she sent some of the dispossessed to kidnap Neil and Paul while they celebrated a successful property deal in an exclusive Michelin-starred Lakeland restaurant. Others, she added, journeyed to Carshalton to fetch me to Morecambe. "You're welcome to stay," she said, "you look like you need somewhere to belong."

"I would be delighted," I replied. "I feel like I've been sleepwalking all these years. Thank you - I feel I can now carve out a future for myself."

"Even if we did carve up the other two," Anna quipped, and we laughed heartily.

It's funny how it has turned out.

Having discovered that The Inedibles' two founding members weren't so inedible after all, and that the band's two chewed-up vegetarians were quite willing to compromise their convictions to dine on the charred remains of their capitalist overlords, we agreed that the time was right to recruit a couple of new members from the Morecambe dispossessed and to get the band back together.

I found the sea air to be greatly inspirational and I have almost finished writing the comeback album; not Defrosted, as stipulated in Neil and Paul's business plan, but a title taken from what I shouted to the crowd that day at the barbecue, "Cannibal-Anarchy".

So yes, I'm looking forward to the reunion.

The tour looks interesting, and it's going to be fun to get back on the road. Some people would rightly question whether Cannibal-Anarchy was part of Neil and Paul's original business plan, but now you know what went into its making,

I'm sure our fans will see it for what it is - a natural progression from their cannibalistic capitalist values and a focus on the band's creative, anarchic core.

I'm sorry, that went on for a lot longer than expected. You have been very patient. I'm sure you're starving by now. Shall we order?

HOw did CiViLiSed SOCiety TUrN iNtO SuCh a ChaOtiC mess?

In this collection we've heard stories from marginalised people, powerless people, people at the bottom of the pile. Let us turn now to another little-heard section of society - the technical middle classes. Pity this comparatively affluent strata as it grinds its way towards retirement - wage slaves to company shareholders, combining long working hours with low cultural input/output. In this story our hero goes underground, meets their past and emerges rejuvenated to, yep, reform the band.

Many people will wonder how I went from punk rocker to civil engineer, from anarchy, peace and freedom to delivering infrastructure for one the region's principal contractors. How, for example, I adjusted to the different pace of life. From making a chaotic racket in a band to delivering major schemes on time and to budget. Well, I didn't. And below I have noted, as accurately as memory will allow, how I came to realise I had chosen the wrong path in life, and how I got myself back on the right road.

On the day in question, we were tendering for a road-building job on the outskirts of Bolton. It would be a straight forward project for us - 2km of offline dual carriageway with a tie-in to existing highway at either end and two structures; a road bridge and a footbridge over a canal. Unusually for us, we conducted the site visit on the same day as the kick-off meeting. To anyone else, this would make perfect sense, but to our fragmented business with its egos and its petty fiefdoms, things rarely went so efficiently. On this occasion, with diary commitments, annual leave and (shock, horror) a tight deadline to consider, our director, Michael Taylor, conceded and we put Tuesday aside to winning work.

The job was design and build, and we were going in with the

same designer as the Stockport job - they were slow and lazy, and had driven Michael up the wall. But all designers had that effect on him; some kind of contractor/designer culture clash. So better the devil you know I suppose.

An interesting aspect to this scheme, and something Michael was sure could win us the job, was that around 1km of the road was to be built on top of raised ground, which was formed from a disused railway track. Ground stabilisation was, of course, a major issue as this part of the scheme was formed from railway ballast, which may have been subject to slippage over the years, and the tender documents did not clearly establish whether adequate ground investigation had been conducted prior to the issue of the documents. Michael made slow work of this in the morning's kick-off meeting, and discussed in length possible ground stabilisation techniques and subcontractors who specialised in each type.

Another interesting aspect, for me anyway, was that the road was to be built through a former industrial area, which had been left derelict for 30 years; nature had taken its course and it had become a wildlife reserve. Pits caused by coal mining activity had filled with water to become home to wildfowl, while many of the trees to the west of the site had preservation orders on them. A local nature group had produced a comprehensive report of flora and fauna in the area, and we would be required to liaise with them throughout delivery of the scheme. I confess that I particularly looked forward to talking to the wildlife experts.

This didn't impress Michael, however. He had lorded it over the morning's meeting flanked by his two acolytes - Dan his commercial manager, and his protigee the golden boy, Glen. The three men had previously worked together before their company was swallowed by a larger contractor. When Michael moved over to our firm, he hired his two former colleagues to replicate his former company's standards and procedures, although it often alienated those of us already working here. Since Michael's arrival, many people had sought positions with other companies.

If company procedures had been adhered to, Nick the bid

manager would have chaired the meeting. But having deferred
to his senior, he hardly got a word in all morning. So, as usual
in these situations, he sat on his hands and stared off into
the middle distance, while the three of them spoke in length
about how they'd delivered similar schemes for their former
company. They also spent the meeting talking disparagingly
about the local authority client, nimby local residents,
interfering neighbouring businesses - anyone who they
anticipated would impede their delivery of the job, or was
likely to kick up a fuss while they were onsite.

"I presume there will be some public liaison work over the
environmental protection works," Glen tactfully suggested
expecting a full-blown response from his boss.

"Fucking tree huggers," Michael bawled across the room. "If we
get in there early enough, we can clear some vegetation before
the soil-strip. It'll cut a few weeks off the programme."

Having spent the previous evening poring over the
environmental report, I ventured to put my twopenn'orth into
the meeting: "The environmental report is comprehensive,"
I said. "There's the possibility of newts in the adjoining
wetland, and badger sets beside the farmland. And bats of
course. We'll require some input from Environmental into the
tender."

This caused even more consternation, as I knew it would,
and set them off about how much time and money was wasted
on protecting newts. Dan, who was strongly opinionated on
countryside issues, suggested that we should exterminate the
badgers.

Like Rob, who by now had glazed over, I slipped into a dream-
world of my own. I let the meeting pass by, dissecting a novel I
had been reading on the train, while Michael and his acolytes
pulled the tender apart to see how best to screw the client.
Anything they saw that wasn't 100 per cent fixed could be put
into a "compensation event". This would be at an additional
cost to the client; or in other words the local authority, in
other words the taxpayer, in other words you and me. I couldn't
wait to get back on the train and return to my book just

to shut out the immorality of what we were actually doing;
taking money from the public purse and putting it into the
company directors' and shareholders' pockets. But that, as I
have been told on numerous occasions throughout my adult
life, is how the world works. We are where we are.

Due to the late cold snap, the site was frozen over. I got a
lift over with Chris who would plan the job and Paul who was
going to price it. We had little in common, other that that
Michael would regularly subject the three of us to the hair-
dryer treatment, and we had formed a mutual trust in which
we got along quietly with one another. When we parked up at
the north end of the scheme, we crossed some trampled wire
fence onto where the job would be, and to where Michael and
his acolytes had unfolded the drawings on big sheets of A2,
which flapped in the breeze. Each had his suit trousers tucked
into his site boots, along with a fluorescent jacket and white
hardhat. I often wondered that if contractors up and down the
country look the same, act the same, probably think the same,
then why bother putting the work out to competitive tender,
when each team bidding for the work is a carbon copy of the
other? Isn't it a serious waste of time, money and resources
when a local authority could have directly employed these
people without handing money to the middle men? And an
outside contractor is far less accountable than a public-owned
organisation; from what I'd seen, they behave how they want,
and charge what they want, and there is little way for the
ordinary person - the person whose money is being spent - to
fully know what they get up to, let alone have any control of
works conducted in their local community.

As I said above, I've been told many times that this is how the
world works. As they say, "It is what it is." And some years ago,
I tried to accept that it isn't going to change just because I
don't like it. I tried to convince myself that I could still be
the person I really was and hold down a day job, and I tried
hard to accept that life inevitably involves a compromise.
But working here meant long hours, long commutes and often
spending time away from home to visit remote construction
schemes. After a brief time, I found it had robbed me of
whatever creativity I thought I would reserve for my free
time. Each day I'd crawl out of work without the energy or the

desire to do what I really felt was worth doing. After a couple
of years, I'd even forgotten what it was that I wanted to do.
I stopped going to gigs, which since leaving school had been
a major part of my life. And I lost touch with many of the
people I knew through that scene. Playing in a band was now a
distant memory and the thought of it was as absurd as saying I
wanted to go and live on Mars. So there I stood beside a stretch
of derelict post-industrial wasteland, on a frozen afternoon
in March, contemplating the futility of what I was doing, and
wanting to get on the train and lose myself in a good book for
an hour.

Michael must have snook up on me while I was lost in thought,
because I snapped back to reality with him shouting down my
ear, "Wakey fucking wakey. I don't pay you to stand there and
look at pretty flowers."

"Wha?" I came out of my trance confused and a little resentful
that I was back in this waking limbo. "There aren't any flowers
Michael, it's winter."

"What are those then?" He kicked at a clod of earth, through
which emerged the heads of snowdrops. He was right. He was
always right. Every time. And that was the problem with him -
there was no arguing with Michael.

We were joined by Florion, who was going to lead the design
team. He'd missed the morning's meeting, but surprisingly
he had been waiting here in his car when we arrived. As a
designer, Florion looked more casual and relaxed than the
shirt-and-tie-wearing engineers - designers always do. They
think they still have a spark of creativity in them, an
artistic flair, which of course the contractors ridicule and
bitterly resent.

The others had set off up the slope and onto the raised
railway track. We had 2km to walk and Michael and his acolytes
were keen to inspect the site of the canal bridge, which they
reckoned contained additional hidden costs for the client.
They'd got a stride on and their fat tummies stuck out like
they were parading across a golf course. I hung back to chat
with Chris.

"I'd tread carefully if I were you mate," Chris said to me in a hushed tone, "he'll have it in for you if you're not careful."

"Don't I know it," I replied, "I'm surprised I didn't die of boredom in the kick-off meeting. Christ that was dull. Did you see how they ran roughshod over Nick!"

"Best keep out of it mate," Chris said. "No good will come of it. Hey, is that one of the culverts?" Chris pointed to a sizeable concrete structure which emerged from beneath the sidings - big enough for a person to stand in. Out of it ran a brook, which flowed towards the ponds across to the east.

"Looks like it," I said. "Bigger than it looked in the drawings."

"Let's go and inspect. It'll get us out of the way for a little while and keep you out of trouble too."

Considering the ground was still frozen, there was quite a strong discharge of water coming out of the concrete box, which was large enough to feature a walkway on one side for access and inspection. Chris said the brook posed a risk of flooding during the construction phase, which may impact on the programme, and it could also present possibilities of undermining the ground above.

He scrambled down to have a look. Chris might have been pushing retirement age, but he was short and stocky, and built like a terrier - just right for this kind of work.

Turning, he said, "Watch yourself on the slope, it's a bit icy. Don't want to be fishing you out of the brook. Not in this weather."

"Yeah, I can just see Michael's face," I replied. And then putting on my Michael voice, which is always a big hit with my colleagues, I added: "Fucking swimming! Do I pay you to go fucking paddling on my time?"

The walkway was navigable and there was nearly enough height to stand fully erect. "Looks like some kids have been down here," Chris said above the roar of the brook, which echoed off the culvert walls, and he nodded over to some graffiti on the opposite side.

But guess what? I don't know how they did it, but some enterprising young soul had crossed this lively waterway and sprayed on the wall, "UK Subs".

The UK Subs were one of the most formative bands of my teenage years and there they were, right there, spray-painted on the wall of an underground waterway. The letters had faded with time, but there it was, still legible - UK Subs. And of all the bands for which you'd risk your life spray-painting a culvert wall above a gushing waterway, the Subs? That was some commitment from the artist.

"Do you know this band then?" Chris called back from further up the culvert, when he heard me whooping with surprise.

"Too right," I called. "Wow, if someone's sprayed that on the wall, it probably dates it to the late 1970s or early 1980s. They enjoyed a few years in the charts, before dropping out of the mainstream after their fifth album."

"What about these then?" he called back. "The Exploited?" Yep, having risked their life to immortalise the Subs on the wall of this underground concrete structure, some young punk had thrown The Exploited into the bargain. And good on them, I thought, you can't fault their bravery.

The third band name sprayed on that wall was the one that knocked me for six. Some unexpected graffiti that got me questioning where life had taken me and which pulled it all round again. The years spent working futile hours for the likes of Michael, of getting home too knackered to think, of worrying about mortgages, pensions, insurance, redundancy, death; anything that dragged me away from the real me. All this being a square peg in a round hole, succumbing to the will of others. Compromise. It was that moment when I set out on a new path, when I read the third and final entry from some distant teenager's punk rock hall of fame.

Just two words on the wall opposite.

And those two words were the name of our band way back when.
The band we'd started after we left school and stuck with for a
few brief years, but which I looked back on after all this time
and wished I were there again. Away from this drudgery. Away
from pretending to be someone that I wasn't. Away from this
futile march towards retirement and death. Away from having
to care. Our band name sprayed in massive letters - even bigger
than the other two.

"Chaotic Mess."

Chaotic Mess started as a joke, a noisy reaction to the
over-produced, over-packaged, over-hyped, but completely
underwhelming chart music which the other kids at school
were into. We hated it - all that posturing and preening,
stupid hair, stupid clothes, falsetto voices, idiotic Radio
1 DJs, miming on Top of the Pops, the vacuity of the music
industry, the pretentiousness of the music press, the blatant
manipulation of the pop charts, the whole insincerity of pop
music.

So we formed Chaotic Mess.

People considered us to be a punk band, but the truth was that
we were only "punk" because we couldn't play our instruments.
We didn't dress like punks, in fact we went out of our way to
avoid doing so. Which probably made us more punk in some
people's books.

Funnily enough, we played quite a few gigs in our short
existence, attaching ourselves to the bottom of the bill on
whatever local gig we could gatecrash. We'd blow eardrums and
scramble brains with breakneck drumming, rumbling bass and
searing feedback before the real bands came on. Our lyrics
covered important issues for us, like nose-picking, farting and
going to the offy. And strangely, we'd get people turning up to
see us, even if they considered us to be a joke band. Which we
were. And we didn't mind if they just came along to heckle us
before the serious bands came on - we encouraged it. And the
headline bands liked us because we made them look competent.
Even if they were shit. Every gig we played was a chaotic mess.

It's a shame we never made it into the studio, as it would
have been good to have had a clear recording of what we were
doing. But we did record a few practice tapes, and these did the
rounds, a few tracks even snook onto compilations. Strangely-
enough, I saw on the internet someone put out a bootleg EP of
one of our noisy practices, and even more weirdly, people cited
us as being a "lost band". I don't know about that, but I was
impressed to hear the bootleg was also released on a Japanese
label. Ha, imagine Chaotic Mess big in Japan! Imagine touring
Japan.

Imagine.

Chris turned around and inched along the walkway back
towards me. "Bloody hell," he said, "it will be a chaotic mess if
we don't get back up there. Come on, you lead the way and let's
see where they're up to. At least we can tell them about the
flood risk - it could impact on the programme. That'll keep
them off our backs for a bit."

We emerged from the culvert and followed the brook down
towards the larger of the ponds, where we could see Paul by
himself, far away from where the others stood on the disused
railway track debating ground stabilisation techniques.

"Looks like a flood risk," I said to him as we approached.
"Could impact on the programme."

But Paul wasn't listening. He was staring out over the pond,
which stretched a couple of hundred yards across the plain.
Trees and tangles of Buddleia had grown around it and we
could see wildfowl where the surface had yet to ice over.
"That's a little grebe fishing over there," he muttered almost
to himself.

"Are they rare?" I asked.

"Not really, but there'll be fish in there," he said. "Something
for them to eat. Shame this is going to be a construction site
in a couple of months." Neither myself nor Chris responded, but
instead stood quietly beside Chris and tried to make out what
he was looking at.

Nick trampled noisily over the frozen earth towards us, his site boots crunching the frosty ground. "We were just looking at the pond and the brook," I said in greeting. "Looks like a flood risk - could impact on the programme."

Nick ignored my comment, and said, "Bloody hell, it's all kicking off up there. Michael's got a right cob-on with Florion. Best keep out of the way." Michael and Florion had different and equally ridgid opinions about ground stabilisation; Florion had decided some sections of the raised track required an expensive option of contiguous piling to stop them from slipping. Michael, rightly in this case, said he was jumping the gun as there hadn't yet been a comprehensive ground investigation. He had explained that we'd price for cement-bound stone columns, but that we would sting the client for additional work once we'd established who carried the risk, should anything hold-up the programme.

This had stirred up some old antagonisms which stemmed from the Warrington job and an argument over who was to blame for programme delays, which had arisen from a similar issue on some loose, sandy ground. This had impacted greatly on our already slim profit margin when the client initiated penalty clauses for the late-running work. And to add to that, the local papers picked up on it and had a field day. "Road to Nowhere", one of the headlines ran. Another read: "Is this the end of the road for local improvements scheme?" You get the picture. Michael was not happy with it at all.

Silhouetted against the skyline, we could see Michael and Florion standing off against each other, while Michael's acolytes stood by and watched. Both men were shouting, but we couldn't make out what was being said.

"My money's on Michael," I said to my three companions.

"I wouldn't disagree with you," Nick replied, "but after this morning's debacle, I hope Florion puts up a decent fight."

"Florion's got the height," Chris added, "but as the saying goes, it's the size of the fight in the dog, rather than the size of the dog in the fight."

And then Michael lunged at Florion. We could see him get the taller man in a headlock and pull him down to hip height, while Michael's acolytes shouted for him to leave it; neither daring to actually step in and separate them. The two adversaries were transfixed for a moment against the steel-grey sky, and I could hear Nick's mirth muffled within his gloved hand. But then courage got the better of Dan and Glen and they dragged Michael away from the other man.

"Come on," Chris said quietly, "there's an interesting location for a site compound over there. I think we should all investigate."

"Yep," agreed Paul. "Move along, nothing here to see."

In silence, the four of us trooped towards a strip of Tarmac we could see a few hundred yards further along the track and near to the canal. None of us wanted to talk about what we'd just witnessed. At least not while Michael and his lackeys were in the vicinity. We'd all long-since learned that you had to be partially blind and hard of hearing if you wanted to stay in this job.

Chris was right about the compound though - it was a sizeable hard-standing area, which looked like it had previously been used as a car park for a neighbouring industrial unit. "Plenty of room for a couple of cabins," he said. "Either as a main compound or satellite."

We could see the group on the track descending the slope towards us. Michael and Florion had settled their differences and were loudly sharing a joke. Michael patted the designer on the back, while Dan and Glen followed behind, both carrying site plans and looking important. Staring up at them I thought, what a chaotic mess.

Later, I waited for a bus to take me to the railway station. None of the others were driving back into town; the roads were busy with the school run and not one of them had volunteered to go out of their way to drop me off. This didn't bother me too much, as I couldn't wait to get away from them.

It took me just over an hour to get home. I didn't read much, and I ignored my phone. I wanted some space, to clear my head of work. But later, when I did check my phone, I had a text from Bob, a fellow surviving member of Chaotic Mess, to say he'd be back in town over the weekend and would I be around?

How was that for cosmic intervention? I'd like to say it was the kind of random resolution that put paid to such a day, but myself and Bob had stayed close all these years and for him to get in touch was nothing unusual.

But do you know what I texted back? Yeah, you guessed it: "Fuck it mate, bring your guitar and let's get the band beck together."

"Chaotic Mess!!!" he texted in reply. "We were awful. Had a bad day mate?"

"Tell you later."

Call Of Duty

In which our hero returns to a Brexit-ravaged Britain to reconnect with an old friend amid a maelstrom of emotion. Set around 2017 when people wouldn't shut up about bloody Brexit - like they understood a single damn thing about the European Union, the historical plight of the British working class (and who the real enemies are), or how democracy works. Hold on tight folks.

It took just two words to ruin my day. Two measly words.

God knows what time Robbie got up, perhaps he'd stayed up all night celebrating. But he texted while I was still asleep. And don't forget, the UK is an hour behind us. In many ways the UK is several decades behind us - it's somewhere I try to avoid. I set my smartphone to flash up a picture of a baboon if Robbie ever rang again so I'd know not to answer, and then I forgot how to change it back. So my phone flashed a baboon with a big red bottom when I looked before getting Ella ready for school.

Just two words: "He's awake."

Considering he'd become such a keyboard warrior of late, the fact that he could get my mind working overtime with just two words, and ruin my day, was good going even for Robbie. We hadn't fallen out, and in recent years he had been my only connection with the past, but as we got older I became increasingly annoyed at his conservative views and I maintained a healthy distance from him.

And guess what? I was happy in Berlin.

I kind of drifted a bit after Duty imploded. I moved away, mostly because I was so bored with where I was living and because there was nothing to do. There were a few bands around, but people mostly spent their time and money going to the pub. I looked round and thought, what a waste of life. Eventually I got myself onto a degree course, scraped a Desmond - that's a 2:2, after Desmond Tutu. You know the South African guy? The anti-apartheid campaigner? Maybe you're too young.

After that I got myself on a PGCE - that's a one-year teaching course. I dunno, I taught in a secondary school for a couple of years, but I wanted a change. Really, it was getting together with Karin that gave me what I was looking for. We met of all places in Kopi. I was visiting Berlin, and just watching a few bands. It was just a gig. But within six months, I handed in my notice and moved over to live with Karin.

I love it here - there's loads of great stuff going on if you're into art and music and the food is great. We have a daughter, Ella, and the schools are so much better than in the UK. I got plenty of time off work on paternity leave while Karin carried on with her career. Could you do that in the UK? I couldn't imagine moving back now. Why would I? The standard of living and the attitude to work/life are so much better over here.

Yeah, Stu. Well, Robbie texted me to say he'd woken up. Stu went into a coma sort of thing in the mid 1990s. He just didn't wake up one day. Imagine that. One of his housemates found him when they hadn't seen him emerge from his room for a while. The doctors didn't really have a name for it, but he showed all the symptoms of life, so they put him on a drip and cared for him until he came round. Crazy. When Stu fell asleep, John Major was in government and they were still talking about the Criminal Justice Bill. Stu slept through the whole Cool Britannia thing, Euro '96, the death of Princess Diana, the Tony Blair government, 9/11, the invasion of Iraq, smartphones, social media, the emerging Chinese economy, the financial crisis of 2008, David Cameron's Big Society, Theresa May's "strong, stable government", the death of David Bowie, and it's been a year and a half since that bloody Brexit vote. He's slept through the lot. There again, you could argue that most of Britain was asleep during that time. The world even.

Well, Duty was a metalcore band we formed with Robbie and a guy called Freddy. I totally unfriended Freddy on Facebook after he started putting up Brexit stuff. I won't go into all of it, but there was this one on his timeline, which showed the white cliffs of Dover with the words, "Fuck off we're full" written beneath it. And there was a photo of him stood in front of a Union Jack in full skinhead regalia trying to look hard. Which he definitely isn't. When we were in a band together, he was one of the most gentle people I knew. Really easy going. I reckon it's living in the same crap town that did it to him. Drinking in the same pub every Friday with the same morons and no-hopers - it's going to have an effect on you. I was really shocked when he started posting that stuff up, but now I'm more sad really. That fucking Robbie isn't much better, but at least he draws the line somewhere.

Duty? Oh yeah, Duty - we were influenced by the stuff coming out of the US, like Cro Mags and Youth of Today. There weren't too many bands playing our kind of metalcore and we carved a name for ourselves. We thought the UKHC scene had been stagnating following an initial surge of interest, and we wanted to do something harder. Something fresh to wake people up. I wasn't keen on the negative side of things, and Robbie's lyrics were too obsessed with violence for my liking, but we did some great shows and toured Europe a couple of times. Bunch of EPs and splits to show for it as well.

Stu kept the band together, especially when we were on tour - he was the one we all got along with. At first it really messed with our heads when he drifted off into that deep sleep, and I attribute it to my own low mood around that time. But some of us sensed a change in attitude in the 1990s and we went off and made something of our lives.

It was great to get an education, and it really broadened my horizons. I started listening to a much wider range of music - Godspeed You Black Emperor, Mogwai, that kind of stuff. These days I'm playing in a darkwave band over in Berlin - you know, kind of post-punk goth stuff. Quite a departure from metalcore, but you've got to move on.

Yeah, so I ignored Robbie's text - I knew he'd want to meet up if I went over and I really didn't have the time, energy or inclination to deal with him. He'd become really obsessed about this whole Brexit thing. Like really opinionated about the European Union, but without understanding a single thing about it. Not wanting to either. He'd try to engage me in discussion, like he wanted to sound off because I was someone he'd known since childhood and I'd chosen a life here in Berlin.

I'd try to tell him about how things were for me, Karin and Ella, but it wouldn't sink into his thick skull. He'd just go on about Brussels bureaucrats telling us what to do. Totally ignoring the fact he was living in a country that repeatedly elected right wing tory governments that blatantly stole from the poor and never gave anything back. Even Blair was at it, although I'd say things were better while he was in. But when I got home from work, my mum called to tell me about Stu and I couldn't ignore it any more.

She told me that she ran into Stu's mum in the Arndale - Stu's mum was shopping for clothes for him. He was awake, but rehabilitating slowly - his muscles had wasted while he was asleep, and he wasn't ready to go out just yet. He was receiving visitors though - Robbie had been round quite a bit and they'd watched films together when Stu felt strong enough. Stu had been asking about me, and his mum had told him all about how I moved out here and that I was still into music despite becoming a dad. Stu said he'd like to see me, and his mum thought it would help with his rehabilitation. I told mum I'd have a chat with Karin and see about getting time away. I could tell she was glad I'd be coming over; we hadn't seen her since Christmas.

Well, me and Karin had a chat and put things in place so I could pop over for a few days - Karin was a rock as always. I booked myself on the Easyjet from Schoenfeld, which was a doddle to get to from here and mum said she'd pick me up at the other side.

But for the two weeks before my visit, Robbie kept texting. At first it was nice stuff like "Stu's been asking after you" and that he was super excited that I was coming over to see him. But as the weeks wore on he began to reminisce about Duty - "Me and Stu talking about those Holland gigs back in the day". It was nice to think back to when we were in Duty, but I have a life and I have a band and I'm happy. "Dug some demos out, been listening to them with Stu." "Fist in the face EP what a killer."

This ground on until a moment that I foresaw but didn't want to face: "Me and Stu reckon we should get the band back

together. You in? Freddy's keen."
I've done that flight a thousand times. Manchester United
were at home, so there were a few footy fans on it - a mix of
expats and football tourists off for the weekend. A bit rowdy
but harmless and pretty genial really. I dunno though, that
journey depresses me.

It's the thought of what's on the other side. It's like England
has a dark cloud over it. The people look so miserable.
Seriously, you can spot them at the airport. Badly dressed,
overweight, pissed. Smug because they think they've got one
over on the rest of the world for having a holiday. Their
expectations are so low, and it's like a race to the bottom
with them. "He's got an extra day's holiday - I don't have one,
so neither should he!" "Why should he have a bonus, when I
don't have one." That kind of mentality. There's no optimism, no
belief that you deserve a decent life, that work doesn't have
to kill you. People get angry with one another but they don't
see the causes of their misery. And art and literature and
film are dismissed as bourgeois activities, not for ordinary
working people. It's like the Haves have a monopoly over their
culture, while the Have Nots are told what to think and what
to feel. The deference they show to those upper class idiots,
and what they let them get away with. I don't get it.

I put a smile on my face when I saw mum waiting for me on
the other side of Immigration. And it was good to see her.
I sometimes wish she'd come and live over here with us, but
her life is here. All her friends, and memories - uprooting
could be too much for her. As we drove out to hers, I began
to fall back in love with the landscape - how everything is
dwarfed by the hills and the majestic lunar landscape of the
moorland. Big and empty and stretching for miles and miles.
You can't help but feel wonder, that no matter what happens,
the hills will be here long after we're gone. Mum was telling
me how bad the moorland fires were in the dry summer, and how
they had to keep the doors and windows closed because of the
pollution. And how these fires might release pollution dating
back to the Industrial Revolution, which had spent a couple of
centuries locked in the peat. Dormant, sleeping.

Stu's mum moved near Stalybridge after she retired, taking

him with her while he was asleep. They set him up in the back bedroom and he slept there all this time. It must have been weird to have been in that house while your son was asleep upstairs for years and years. Just getting on with your life as best you could, and watching the world change while he slept through it all.

He had been such a positive force within the band - drove us forward with his energy and ambition. We played a gig in a pub near Upper Mill once. Loads of people travelled over for it too - it was tightly-packed and pretty raucous. I loved playing local gigs - you got the feeling that you were creating a scene right there on your doorstep. Exerting a positive influence on the world around you. That things might change for the better. Despite Robbie's lyrics about anger, depression and violence. Most of the crowd was straight edge, so the pub didn't do as well as it hoped with a turnout that size. People were having a laugh skateboarding outside, it was great to feel part of that scene.

Upper Mill was a lot quainter than I remembered it. We used to go round there a bit in our early teens and drink cider up in the surrounding hills. We would take a ghetto blaster and listen to Minor Threat overlooking the reservoir. I stopped for a coffee in a place which I guessed was a wine bar in the evening. Mostly, it was older people in there, and they all looked healthy and relaxed. I'm not surprised Stu's mum moved there when she had the chance.

Stu had hardly changed at all. It was probably the Gorilla Biscuits t-shirt that did it. He was propped up in bed when his mum showed me in. He looked pasty-faced, but he'd hardly aged. "So good to see you man." Hearing his voice again, it was like a quarter of a century hadn't happened. Like we'd never been apart. We hugged, and it was a tearful, emotional experience. "I was worried you weren't going to come - I was going to send you a text."

That threw me. "You just woke after 25 years and you've got a mobile phone?" I asked him.

"Yeah, mum got it for me. She said it's how people keep in

touch now. These used to be the size of a shoe box and only used by yuppies." We were looking into each others' eyes while he was talking and it was like a big part of my life had been resolved. All that time, while I was getting a life together, moving away, settling down, still playing in bands and checking out new music, Stu had been there at the back of my mind. Not participating in the world, not growing or developing as a human being. And it gnawed away at me all that time. "Shit man, you've hardly aged," he said. "Life's treating you well."

I told him about Berlin, where I live, family life, the gigs I'd been to and what I was listening to. Like I really wanted to share all this with him. And Stu was lapping it up like he was thirsty for knowledge, to get out there and be a part of the world again. I downloaded some tracks onto his phone so he could check out some new music. Guess who showed me how to do that? Ella - she just instinctively knows how to do this sort of stuff. Kids do.

I told him that we'd got a spare room in the flat and how it would be good for him to come out and stay with us as soon as he was better. He told me about the people who had come to see him in the couple of weeks since he woke up. His sister visited with his niece and nephew. "So strange to see them," he said. "Last time I saw Sarah she was still a child herself. The kids were great, but kids these days just play on their smartphones don't they?"

"More or less," I agreed. Stu told me that Robbie had been round nearly every day, bringing him the newspaper or some music to listen to. He'd been talking a lot about me, and telling him how I got my life together and shipped out to Berlin. When Stu told me this, I kind of felt bad about ignoring Robbie's texts. And then I remembered the life I got away from. I asked Stu how Robbie was doing. "Not as well as you by the looks of things," he said. "When he walked in, I thought it was his dad."

"Yeah, he put a bit of weight on," I agreed. "We're all getting on a bit."

"He sounds like his dad too," Stu continued. "You know how he'd

corner us in his hallway and give us the state of the nation about stuff - about immigrants and trade unions..."
"A lot of people over here seem to have got angry about things," I said. "I can't really work it out."

"Yeah, but when I went to sleep, it was the John Major government, and nothing's changed. If the papers are anything to go by, the tories have got even worse."

I had to agree with him, but I told him to come over to Berlin and see some good stuff happening in the world. Just then, Stu's mum came into the room and told us that Robbie was downstairs and he'd brought Freddie round to see him. "Mum, could you tell him that I'm all peopled out just now," Stu said. "Apologise for me." I told Stu I'd nip off and promised to come round again while I was over. We hugged once more and told each other how good it was to talk again. Genuinely and honestly. Friends reunited.

I wasn't looking forward to meeting Robbie and Freddy as I walked down the stairs. I really wanted to get on the plane back home and not have to deal with them. But Stu's mum collared me. "Thank you for coming all this way," she said, "it means such a lot to Stu. And to me. Would you like to stay for a coffee and say hello to Rob and Freddy?"

I couldn't refuse. How could I tell her these two former friends and bandmates were part of the reason I escaped this country? How the small town mentality, conservative outlook, petty jealousies and vicious talk about vulnerable, voiceless people showed me how defeated I would have been if I'd stuck around. How low my expectations would have been. How narrow my horizons. Yeah, I ran away from here, but I ran away to a better life. I made that choice and I wouldn't be dragged back. Why would I, when I have the life that I have?

But I can't refuse her offer of coffee, so I thank her and ask for no milk. She shows me through to the front room where two fat, middle-aged men with bloated faces and shaved heads wait for me.

Robbie is first. He jumps up and throws his arms round

me. "Fuck, mate, so good to see you," he says. There's genuine
affection in his voice too. "You came all the way over here. You
don't know how much that means to us all. Not just Stu, but me
and Fred too. We knew you'd pull through. You're a true friend."
His sincerity really throws me. This from the man who posted
something about "rats from a sinking ship" beside a news story
about expats' concerns about Brexit. "We all appreciate how
you've got a family over in Germany, Robbie continues, "and for
you to drop everything to come over and see a mate means such
a lot to us." I'm genuinely thrown - one minute I'm expecting to
get into a fight with two skinheads, the next it's turning into
a tearful reunion.

"Yeah, you're a true friend," Freddie chips in from behind
Robbie. He's wearing a short sleeved Ben Sherman, and I give
his arms a quick glance for any dodgy right wing tattoos. But
the only one I can make out is a Curzon Ashton FC badge. Non-
league football, I have to concede, is hardly a stamping ground
for the far right. Or is it?

"Mate, I don't think you two have met in 25 years," Robbie
says, "I give you Mr Frederick Taylor." I'm shaking hands with
Freddie, and he's beaming at me.

"It's been way too long," he says. "You're looking great." So we
sit down in Stu's mum's front room, she brings us coffee and we
chat about our lives. Neither Robbie nor Fred have continued
with bands after Duty, although they've both listened to a lot
of music. Mostly punk. Fred's telling me he's listening to a lot
of streetpunk, which I take for a veiled reference that he's
into skinhead music, and I jokingly tell him so.

"Well, I came at it from all that US stuff in the 1990s," he says,
"and then worked my way back. There were a load of bands that
we missed. And no, I don't tolerate all that racist stuff. When
I come across any of that, I unfriend them on Facebook." Am I
convinced? Have I jumped to the wrong conclusions about this
guy? I reserve some scepticism, but don't want an argument just
now.

They're impressed that I kept on with making music, although
Robbie calls me a goth when I describe my current band. Fred

captains his local darts team, which is a far cry from his straight edge past, and Robbie still gets out to a few gigs. He tells me he got to see Negative Approach play the Star and Garter a year or two back. "Man, you should have been there - they nailed it," he says. "They blew me away. Negative Approach!"

And he then broaches the subject of a reunion. "Look, we know you've got commitments," he says, "but we were thinking of turning it into a benefit gig for Stu. We don't know yet if he'll be well enough to play, but we could find a stand-in and maybe get him up for a couple of songs at the end. It would give him something to aim for as well, to give him some focus while he adjusts to the world."

I'm cringing inside. How can I say "no, fuck off" and get away from these guys? How can I tell them I left them behind a long, long time ago, and I'm only here because I felt a duty to an old friend the world forgot a quarter of a century ago?

"Look, mate," Robbie continues, "you don't have to give us an answer right now. But having you there with us, just for one gig, would mean the world to all of us. It wouldn't be right without you."

I hear myself saying, "I'll think it through and talk it over with Karin when I get back". But how can I refuse? It would be for just one gig, as Robbie says. No more. And then I can safely put the episode with Stu behind me. We can all move on. Get on with our lives and carve out a future for ourselves.

I leave them in Stu's mum's front room to warm embraces and kind words, and promise Stu's mum I'll be round again before I take the plane home. Freddie offers me a lift, but I say I'd like time to think - it has been a big day for all of us.

It's going to be difficult to explain to Karin how I've decided to do a reunion gig with Duty. Especially after the way I've talked about these guys all this time. But only a fool doesn't know when to change his mind. It's my duty.

And Karin will understand, she's a rock.

Silent Minority

In which our strong, silent protagonist, having deftly avoided the dead-ends, the cul-de-sacs and the trappings of conservative life, finds themself cornered to have inflicted upon them the minutiae, the tedium, the boring detail and the narrow, airless, dimly-lit aspirations of ordinary fucking people.

"So, what are you up to these days? Married? Kids? Work?"

"Fuck marriage, fuck having kids and above all else, fuck work. I won't define myself on those terms."

"Tell me about it, I'm starting to wonder about all that too. We've got three kids, all in their teens. None of them are into punk mind, they just think I'm a daft old sod for still listening to all the old stuff. But come on, those records are classics and you've got to agree, the punk years were the best of our lives. Weren't they? A lot of people just see it all as a phase we went through. Ange, my wife, she got out of it after she had our first. She has to put up with me listening to all my records and CDs. And yes, to be honest, it took second place for a few years while I grew the business, well we've all got to make a living haven't we? And raising kids isn't cheap is it? Oh, yeah, I forgot you don't have kids. But still time, eh? We've still got a few years in us. Just look at Charlie Chaplain, he was in his 70s. But I've got to say, raising kids isn't cheap, I can tell you. So there was a good 10 or 15 years when I lost touch with it all, and I stopped going to gigs. I'm sure it happened to you for a while. You know when you still like the music, but you don't have the time to do all the things you did back then. But I'll tell you what, all I want to do now is get back into it. Seriously, I mean, what's important in life? I look back to then and how we used to be and I think, yes, that's how it should be. All the time. I mean, we don't have the same energy we used to have, and neither of us has the hair. But I just love that music. That's why me and Flea got the band back together. It was after Mark's funeral last year. Did you know he died? Pretty grim really, but not unexpected. Didn't come as a shock to anyone. It was in the paper and everything. It's his family we felt sorry for, having to cope with the aftermath. Picking

up the pieces and carrying on. And then Tim Lewis got married
to Jo. Took them a long time to get together. But they got there
in the end. Don't tell me you haven't got your eye on an old
flame. Who was that one you used to hang about with? Sally?
You should see what she's up to. It's easy to get back in touch
these days with the internet and all that. That's one thing
that all that stuff with Mark taught us - life's too short. So
Tim and Joanne tied the knot just after Mark's funeral. Quite
fitting really. You should have come along. I know you and Tim
didn't see eye to eye back then. I remember you were always
at each other's throats. But there's been a lot of water under
the bridge since then, and he would have been made up to
have seen you. Honestly. We all would have been. Seeing us all
together, it was just like back then; there were loads of old
faces. Even Nick, remember him? His missus has got him right
under her thumb. He rarely ever comes out with us these days.
Oh, you might know her - Becca? She was around back then. They
got hitched years ago. He's still got his electrical business. She
went off and got a degree, but they're still together. We got
this younger lad in on vocals - you probably don't know him,
Steve? Other Steve - Steve Cahill - went all weird, he stopped
going out and shrunk in on himself. He went off for a bit,
and when he came back he didn't want to come out with any
of his old mates any more. I think that's wrong - you've got to
remember your roots. You've got to know who your friends are.
Steve Cahill got right out of punk. I don't think he listens
to it any more. Shame really, I think it's a part of who you
are, all the old stuff. He's in some electro band as well. Not
interested in getting the band back together at all. I mean, it
wasn't going to be a full-time thing for any of us, what with
family and work and all that. Just a bit of fun. Something
to do. You know, playing the stuff that you really care about.
And we've got Mike here on guitar. It felt strange picking up
a bass again; I didn't play it for about 15 years, well after we
had our first, but Flea kept on nagging me to take it up again,
until I gave in. I thought, why not? Why the fuck not? The
business pretty much runs itself and I mean, what's important
in life? It felt right, playing our old songs again and we went
down really well at Tim and Joanne's wedding. Probably better
than back in the day. So we carried it on, just a bit of fun.
We rent a studio space in town. Much better than we had back
then. That old garage. Freezing in the winter, and boiling hot

in the summer. Remember how we all used to cram into it. I
don't know how we got anything done. It would be nice to get
a few more gigs. We will have a bit more time on our hands
now the kids don't need driving about so much. And they'll be
off to university in a year or two, so we'll have the place to
ourselves. I'm surprised you never got hitched. What happened
to that one you were seeing? What was her name? Spanish
girl. She was quite a looker. I don't mind saying we were all
impressed when you turned up with her. Pity it never worked
out. But that's life isn't it? You will have to come and see us
when we get a few gigs. It would be just like old times. And it
would be great to have a few familiar faces down the front.
You never know, you might bump into Sally - take up where you
left off. Or come along to our rehearsal studio. You'd be well
impressed. Let us know if you can get time off work and just
come down. Where are you working at the moment anyway?"

"Like I said, fuck marriage, fuck having kids and above all
else, fuck work. I won't define myself on those terms."

TueSday iS NOT SOYLENT Green day

If we learned anything in the 21st Century, it's that the truth is a flexible friend...

First published in One Way Ticket to Cubesville #21 (2018)

So... how is it that a couple of songs we wrote in our crappy school band sold millions of records, which made some people very rich, but nobody wants to listen to my story and there's nothing I can do about it? Tell me. How is it?

Well, I've got the band back together, and when I'm out of here I intend to play those songs. Let them take me to court for it. OK, neither of the other original members have agreed to join me, but I'm happy to go acoustic if needs be, just to get it out there.

No way am I backing down on this, you hear? No way.

Where to start? The beginning sounds good to me.

Me, Anthony "Wristwatch" Gilbert and Wayne "Stretchmarks" Mortimer (aka The Blob) were the school nerds; we were shit at football and we weren't even clever. No-one wanted to know us and the girls, especially, hated us. The only thing we had was music; we would sit round at each other's houses drinking tea and talking music all night; Black Flag, Crass, Dead Kennedys - in many ways we were ahead of our peers.

But that' didn't matter at our school - everyone hated the music we liked, which in turn made them hate us even more. So after many, many nights listening to music, the three of us had an idea of starting a band. We were going to be a kick-ass punk rock band and would make everyone at school take notice of us. What did we have to lose? How could our situation possibly be any worse than it already was?

I had some ideas for songs from listening to old first wave
7"s and with me on guitar, Stretchmarks on bass and Tony
behind the drums we set about practising in Stretchmarks's
mum's garage once she'd moved the Saab out of the way. Word got
around school that we had a band and, with the headmaster
chronically short of inspiration to fill a bleak half hour of
assembly other than with uniform checks and sermons about
tolerance, charity and accepting one another as equals, we
were booked to play.

Four weeks of practising later and we had three songs - enough
to fill our slot in the assembly on the Tuesday morning. We
actually sounded pretty good. Not as good as the old Cockney
Rejects or UK Subs records we'd been listening to, but we were
musically astute enough to put a rocky edge on some of the pop
punk coming out of the US at the time like the Descendants
and Dag Nasty, and with that we were pretty confident when we
took to the stage that Tuesday morning.

Tuesday, incidently, was what we'd decided to call our band -
after the line in one of our favourite sci-fi films, Soylent
Green starring Charlton Heston and Edward G Robinson - the
one where they found out they were eating people, like what
happened to that band The Inedibles, "Tuesday is Soylent Green
day." Goodbye nerd-dom, and a big hello to Ruby Tuesday, let the
good times roll. But you've guessed it already - that's not how
the story ended. Not at all.

We hadn't even endured five minutes of laughter, booing and
missiles before the headmaster showed mercy on us and pulled
the plug. The crowd had instinctively rounded on us nerds
and now our hopes to be liked and respected were dashed at
our feet - we actually came out of the episode less popular
and with even more hurtful nicknames than before. So we gave
it up and never looked back. That was the end of our band,
Tuesday.

OK, cut to a few years later when I'm working in a pub in
Manchester during the Madchester renaissance. I've left those
losers Tony and Stretchmarks far behind and I'm living the
life of Riley just checking out as many bands and clubs as
I can. That's when I'm not working in the bar, which is a few

weeknights and most weekends. One night I get talking to a couple of American kids about the British punk scene - they're really interested in the music and know it inside out. It's about half an hour before I knock off and they invite me to go along to a party with them. Some time during that night I pick up a guitar and strum out some Tuesday songs from all that time ago - I remember playing them Bastard Case, and a song I wrote about neo-conservativism hitting a small farming village on the edge of Merseyside. I called it American in Lydiate. These kids loved them and I think someone taped me playing. I was well on form. Great night, great people.

A few more years pass and I'm driving a taxi for a living. While I'm waiting for a booking to get their arse into gear I stick on the radio to relieve the tedium. Well fuck me my song American in Lydiate comes on the radio. Radio 1 too! "Don't wanna be an American in Lydiate."

The song that I tried to play in assembly all those years before. It's almost word for word, note for note. I didn't want to get in touch with the other band members - Tony still lives with his mum and Stretchmarks thinks I'm an asshole. He's right, but he's an asshole too.

So I get in touch with the record label and ask them what's going on. After some time, I get some smartass US lawyer threatening to counter-sue me if I continue with my enquiries. So, like with the school band, I let it go and try not to let the crushing defeat hang even heavier on my already crap life.

But this band I keep hearing on the radio - against the odds it looks like an actual punk band is on its way up. And very soon they become what we'd dreamed of all those years ago - they're written about in the papers, constantly played on the radio and get regular spots on the TV. People think they're cool and ordinary people, not just losers like us, start wearing their t-shirts.

So after another few years of living in a miserable post-industrial backwater, a couple of failed relationships and a few visits to the doctor for depression, I get it together to go to one of their shows to confront them about stealing my songs. I heard they were playing in a massive arena - can you believe a punk band playing in an arena? The Pistols had to reform to get that kind of interest.

At the concert, there's a real mix of ages, but there's a guy in the next seat who is only a few years younger than me. Finally, after the lame-ass mediocre support acts, the band comes on and launches straight into their version of American in Lydiate. "This is my song!" I yell above the opening verse. "Yes! It's mine too!" the guy next to me yells back - he's grinning like an idiot and attempting to high-five me. Asshole. "You thieving bastards," I scream from the cheap seats in Row Z at the back of the arena, "give me my fucking royalties."

A balding geography teacher accompanying his tousle-haired son turns round from the seats in front of me. "Hey, do you mind keeping the language down," he says nodding to the small kid in an oversized tie-dyed sweatshirt beside him.

"Gooooood evening Manchester, it's so good to be back." It's him - the guy from the party who got me to play the songs for him after the pub that night. I was drunk and flattered and let him fucking tape it. I remember his name now - Billie Joe, and his friend Mike is playing the bass. Oh fuck - now I get it, they've named their group after the same line in the Charlton Heston film we used to watch - "Tuesday is Soylent fucking Green Day".

"Give me my fucking money shitface!" I yell. I've given geography teacher a shove in the back while I'm shouting at the band.

Well, I'm sick of it. I'm sick of scraping a miserable living. Sick of losing at school. Sick of losing at life. Sick of shit housing, poxy wages and failed miserable relationship after failed miserable relationship. Sick of being told what to do by JobcentrePlus. Sick of being thrown out of pubs for being too drunk. Sick of arguing with my twattish neighbours. Sick of what might have been. Sick of what wasn't. Sick of being bullied and pushed around. Sick of being a nobody. Sick of damp grey streets full of downtrodden sullen-faced losers like me. I'm sick of it.

"What do you want to hear Manchester?!? I can't hear you!" Then Billie Joe and Mike launch into my song Bastard Case, which he's renamed Basket Case:

"That's my fucking song you asshole!" I'm raving by now. "That's my fucking music." There's a crowd of angry parents round me and I can see some luminous Showsec jackets approaching, which I know from long, bitter experience means an arm up the back, ejection from the side door and a few unkind words as I rapidly negotiate the fire escape steps.

But I just can't take it any more - another roughing up by the bouncers is not going to stop me. I'm jumping around Row Z, waving my arms like a mad thing at the tiny figure of Billie Joe away in the distance. "That's my fucking music. This should have been me. Why are you up there and not me, bastards. Give me my money, fucking...get the fuck off me. Get your fucking hands off me. This should have been me. This should have been Tuesday."

And once again, Tuesday is not Soylent Green day.

ThursdaY BlOOdY ThursdaY

In this frank, yet totally fictitious interview, our protagonists, for protagonists are what they are, come to terms with the break-up of their band and the enormous steps each subsequently took to get the band back together.

Rat: "I've carried the guilt about what happened to Sue with me all these years. I'd say much more than the other two. After all, it was our fault she got sent down for as long as she did, and none of us has really spoken about it. So I can't say how much it means that she wants to get the band back together, to let bygones be bygones and pick up where we left off."

Spike: "Yeah, I've really missed being in a band. And I look back on the time we were together as the happiest of my life. Just the freedom. I wouldn't say me and Sid weren't affected by what happened to Sue as much as Rat, but, you know, we got on with things, moved on like. It's just in the last couple of years that I've really felt it. I never meant Sue any harm, I think I'm right in saying none of us did - she was the one who got us together in the first place."

Rat: "That's right. She was the driving force behind us. She wrote the songs, made the banners, and always pushed for the animal rights agenda. Spike took on the managerial role - doing the merch and booking gigs. You even did that newsletter and the mailout. Remember? And Sid did all the driving bless him. Isn't that right Sid?"

Spike: "Nope. No answer. The quiet thoughtful type. But yeah, to pick up on what Rat was saying, there was a lot of energy in that band, which enabled us to achieve so much in such a short time. What, three years? Seems like five minutes. It was the veal protests that got us together, and look at it all now - veganism is mainstream, and you wouldn't think of treating animals the way they did back then. The world moved on. We all did."

Rat: "For me, the veal protests changed my outlook on life. I turned vegetarian around that time, and recently I turned vegan. I think that decision came from thinking about the band, and missing that scene."

Spike: "For me it was about the people. Really, you met the best people - honest, fun, intelligent. I learned so much in those few years. And I wish I'd stayed with it."

Rat: "The veal protests? I'd seen them on the news. You know, people throwing themselves in front of cattle trucks at Dover and Folkestone. At first I thought they were mad. I couldn't understand why they'd do such a thing. And I was thinking, haven't these people got jobs to go to? Is this all they have to worry about? I guess I thought they were middle class wankers. But I was curious, you know, and started researching it. The protesters belonged to a group called the Society to Abolish Road Veal Exports, or STARVE, and from the news coverage, they looked like concerned liberals and unemployed layabouts. But I remember thinking they were causing quite a stir and I started to read up about it. The company responsible was called Foods UK (FUK), and the road haulage firm that was copping it at the ports was called Transport-Oriented Storage Solutions (TOSS). The newspaper articles carried quotes from the bosses of each about how their treatment of animals was lawful and humane, and how the protesters were putting jobs at risk, blah blah, the usual stuff. It was when the Minister for Agriculture at the time, Piers Fahy, or Lord Birkdale to give him his full title, called for tougher sentences for protestors and more funding for the police to deal with the problem, that I thought, 'Right, I've got to get involved in this.' And within a few months, I'd met Sue, Spike and Sid and we were all in a band together."

Spike: "We jumped quite a bit there. But I can understand that. Yeah, I remember first seeing you at the protest - you had all these crazy dreads and were dancing in front of the coppers. Making a real nuisance of yourself. Taunting them like."

Rat: "Yeah, I don't think I got arrested that day, despite my efforts. I remember thinking you looked really straight.

You'd turned up with your girlfriend at the time, and looked uncomfortable with it all. I think that's why we wanted to include you, to bring you out of your shell. Sue was a great believer in people and brought us all together."

Spike: "Yes. She wasn't just the driving force for the band, she was the glue. I don't think we ever had a proper argument in all the time we were together. We'd just talk it through and reach a consensus. I wish the rest of my life could have been like that. It would have saved a lot of hassle."

Rat: "Wouldn't it. Well the band was there firstly to promote the campaign against the veal trade, but we also campaigned on a wider animal rights platform - hunt sabs, anti-vivisection, fur trade, factory farming - the list goes on. The name Thursday came from a late-night discussion between us that we could name a song for each day of the week - I Don't Like Mondays, Ruby Tuesday, Wednesday Week, Friday on my Mind, When Saturday Comes, Sunday Bloody Sunday - but we couldn't think of one for Thursday. Nothing to do with animal rights at all. And it messed with people's heads on gig listings: 'This Friday, for one night only it's Thursday.'"

Spike: "Musically, we reflected our wide-ranging tastes. I know you were into that whole festival dub scene Rat..."

Rat: "And I always suspected you'd got some Dire Straits records stashed away somewhere. U2 at least."

Spike: "You know what, now we can talk about this openly, and as responsible adults, I can put my hand on my heart and say I wasn't into either. But I do totally fess-up to Elvis Costello. OK, and a lot of mainstream rock. Boston, GnR, bring it on!"

Rat: "Haha. I knew it. Something wasn't quite right from the start. Actually, that 's why the band fell apart. Or mostly why."

Spike: "That day... That rehearsal..."

Rat: "That day. We were rehearsing some new songs. Sue had a load of lyrics and really it was down to me and Spike to write the tunes. I'd been toying with ideas for a reggae number, and

Spike had a few bass lines. Well, I asked you to put one by me and he started to play. I don't know why I said it, just joking really but as soon as those words came out of my mouth, it was like a bomb had dropped."

Spike: "Many a true word said in jest."

Rat: "I hope you don't mind me saying Spike, but the bass line was shit. Not one of your best at all mate. And I told the band as much. But then I said something like, 'We're not a pretend reggae band - it's not like we're The Police or anything.' Fuck me, I knew from the looks on Spike's and Sid's faces I'd hit the mark. Sid went white as a sheet, and Spike, you looked guilty as fuck mate."

Spike: "Haha, you got us well and truly banged to rights. I thought Sid was going to have a heart attack. That right Sid?"

Rat: "Nope, exercising his right to remain silent there. Well, we blustered through the rest of the practice and as usual we trooped off to the pub afterwards. Sue hadn't noticed the exchange between us, and was happy to talk through a few plans for benefit gigs she was organising. She was up for college in the morning so she nipped off about half ten. I remember we'd bagged ourselves a quiet corner, so I got a round in for the three of us and confronted you two."

Spike: "Fuck me, I was bricking it when you went off to the bar. I knew what was coming next."

Rat: "Well, I just came out with it. 'Are you both coppers?' I asked. You just sat there not saying anything."

Spike: "We were waiting to see if you were going to admit to anything yourself. Thankfully, you did."

Rat: "We all knew something was amiss. And I'd had my suspicions about you Spike from day one. Sid was always difficult to read, but I'd clocked the look on his face at the practice, and I'd guessed that seeing as you two arrived on the scene at around the same time, there was a connection between you. So I just said it."

Spike: "It was quite a surprise when you did mate. We knew something was up, but you caught us, pardon the expression, flat-footed."

Rat: "Appropriate turn of phrase there Spike. Well done. So I came out with it, 'I'm a private investigator working for Foods UK. I've been investigating the animal rights movement, and STARVE in particular. I am reasonably sure the both of you are undercover policemen.'"

Spike: "Yep, as I said before, banged to rights. I don't know about Sid, but I was relieved when you came out with it. We knew there was something not quite right about you - your timeline didn't make sense. If I remember, you said you'd been travelling in India at the same time that you said you'd attended an anti-vivisection march. We had our suspicions about you. Private investigator made sense."

Rat: "I'd approached Foods UK when the Minister for Agriculture had been banging on about tougher sentences and more budget. It sounded like Foods UK were willing to pay for some insider information on the protests. When I researched the background, I found our Lord Birkdale was a non-executive director of a subsidiary, Food and Transport (Combined with Allied Trucks Ltd), or FAT(CAT), and I knew they'd appreciate some private sector support."

Spike: "We'd been briefed to anticipate some of your lot, but to treat you like normal protestors. I'm aware of exchanges of information that went high above the heads of us regular foot soldiers. Yeah, myself and Sid had been put in there just after the STARVE protests kicked off. We'd infiltrated a hunt sabs group, coincidentally in Lord Birkdale's Berkshire constituency, and we were moved onto the ports. I don't know if Birkdale had any say in it, but I wouldn't have been surprised."

Rat: "I expected some undercover police presence during the protests, but I must say I was well impressed that you'd infiltrated the heart of the group. You were even booking the venues for the fundraising events, Spike. And Sid, you were driving the van everywhere."

Spike: "It's all been public for a while now, but we were part of the operation known as the Covert Unit for Negating Terrorism."

Rat: "Or 'CUNT'."

Spike: "Unfortunate. We were briefed to get right to the heart of STARVE. And because of her involvement and commitment to the protests, Sue was identified as a target. I'm guessing your employers had told you the same Rat."

Rat: "Sort of. I'd told them I would get in with the ringleaders. But regarding Sue, I just wanted to be in a band. So I was made up when she suggested we start one."

Spike: "Being in a band was great. I had a conservative upbringing - my dad was a copper - and I missed out on a lot of the music that you and Sue listened to. So all these gigs and travelling about the country meeting all these people was a revelation to me. I know I was living a double life at the time, but I think you'll understand Rat when I say it was the best time of my life."

Rat: "I'm totally with you on that point. Finding out that you and Sid were coppers didn't change my mind about those days at all. So when you contacted me out of the blue, as it were, I was really made up."

Spike: "Me and Sid met regularly after the STARVE protests. It was something encouraged in CUNT, even after they disbanded the unit. It gave us all a sense of camaraderie. Even while we were undercover, we'd pop off to a safe house every week and crack open a couple of Carlings with the other undercover lads. Kept us sane."

Rat: "So when you asked me along to one of your little gatherings, I suggested that we got up and played a few numbers together. For old time's sake."

Spike: "Honestly mate, that was such a laugh. Everyone was in character, even those of us who'd been out of it for some years. And there were a load of furrys there - that's what we called the undercover animal rights lads. There was even a mosh pit with them all going ape to our music. I got such a buzz out of it - it was just like old times."

Rat: "I've been in a few bands since then, but there was something special about Thursday. I think you and Sid brought a freshness to it because you were seeing it for the first time. But I missed Sue. We all did."

Spike: "I think we did a good job sharing the vocals. And the furrys loved the animal rights speeches in between songs. They were cheering along to all that 'Meat is Murder' and 'Save the Whale' stuff you were saying Rat. By the time we got to the end they were all chanting A-L-F! A-L-F! Like that, I was welling up inside, and I could see Sid was moved by it too - weren't you Sid?"

Rat: "We all were. To get that kind of reception - how could you not be overwhelmed?"

Spike: "So when the Chief Inspector suggested we play a few more get-togethers and organise events to train the younger surveillance operatives in what it's like to go to a gig, how could any of us refuse?"

Rat: "It was an honour. And to think, we were getting paid to do something we loved as well. I know you two have your generous policeman's pensions to fall back on, but for me it really took the pressure off, financially."

Spike: "I loved watching the raw recruits getting into it. Seeing them loosen up. See them trying to dance, but not quite getting it right. You know - dancing too well. I was the same when I started out - I must have looked a right prat. Hey, we'd have them circle moshing or doing a wall of death by the end though. Great fun."

Rat: "The high point for me was when we played the Secret Policeman's Ball that Christmas - such a gathering of in-character undercover cops! Honestly, there was everyone there, tree huggers, nazi skins, anti-nazi skins, LBGTQ-whatever, black rights, football hooligans, drug dealers - the lot. All partying away. I've never seen such a mixed group of people all enjoying themselves in the same room. You can't beat it."

Spike: "I think we got a bit too carried away with it all. That's how we got found out."

Rat: "It was Pogo's birthday. We should have kept it in-house and held it in a safe space. But it was his 50th and he wanted to splash out. He'd hired a big hall up north. There was food, plenty of alcohol and he'd booked us to play before the disco. Great night."

Spike: "But we got too cocky. By that time, we'd been playing undercover events and security conferences all across Europe, and even a few in the States. We'd forgotten the golden rule - it's a small world."

Rat: "Yeah, you can say that again. It's always the one you don't expect. When you're undercover, you always dread randomly bumping into someone you know. Even your mate's mum just there in the street. It's the same for all of us. You just have to think on your feet. Be prepared, as they say."

Spike: "But some things you can't prepare for... Right, the bar was run by this lovely couple called Jim and Sam. They were from down south, but moved up to the Lakes because they liked hill walking. Got out of the rat race and all that. Pogo would take his real family up there when he was off duty. Well, Jim and Sam had their niece coming up to stay with them that weekend, which they might have mentioned, but none of us was paying attention - we were nervy about playing a big gig. I'm sure you know what happened next..."

Rat: "Yeah, Sue arrived while we were on stage. We didn't see her at all. The first thing we knew, we'd done a couple of encores and we were headed for the bar. There she was with her rucksack at her feet and a face like a stormy winter's night in downtown Windermere."

Spike: "Telling you mate, I nearly had a heart attack. Sid was speechless."

Sue: "Sid was fucking speechless. How the actual fuck do you think I felt having spent three years in prison for incitement, ratted on by my own band mates - two of whom I suspected of being undercover policemen. Rat - I thought you were some moron who couldn't play guitar properly, I asked you to join the band because I took pity on you. But you were the worst of them all. And when I saw you playing MY songs, singing MY lyrics, and having the fucking audacity to make these impassioned speeches about tortured animals murdered on the whims of fashion, I couldn't believe what I was seeing. You twats got me sent down for fuck's sake."

Rat: "Sue, we've apologised and we're truly sorry for what we put you through. We've carried this guilt around with us since we did that terrible thing."

Spike: "Same from me Sue. And Sid. It took someone as big-hearted as you to put that behind them. And we're truly thankful that you've given us a second chance."

Sue: "Well, seeing you there together on stage did bring it back to me. I'd spent a few years just wandering, without a sense of purpose. And I did love being in a band with you. Even if you are a bunch of shits. I think it was because you were so hopeless. I'd been in other bands before Thursday, and they were quite good. Musicians who could actually play. Could write songs. Had a stage presence. Believed in what they were doing. You had none of those things. Looking back, it's so obvious that Spike and Sid were policemen. You had such crap punk names. Your real names are Laurence and Matthew for crying out loud. But Pogo, Rat and the rest - come on! And you didn't have an ounce of musical ability between you. When Rat said he suspected Spike of possessing Dire Straits records earlier, I had to laugh. I had him down for a Bryan Adams fan."

Rat: "The night of that gig was such a revelation for us. It brought it all out into the open and it allowed us to get on with our lives."

Sue: "So aunty Samantha and uncle James kept the bar open and we stayed up talking late into the night. It was good to finally get some answers from the guys; I had a good idea about the truth but... I told them how I had just wandered for a few years. How, like Rat, I went travelling to India. It's surprising our paths didn't cross - as he said before, it is a small world. I got a nine-to-five office job for a while, but that didn't suit me. I guess I'm not cut out to be a regular citizen. But I couldn't go back to the animal rights movement, I was without a home."

Rat: "We were so made up when you told us you'd turned Queen's evidence against the other protestors - made a deal for a shorter sentence. You'd crossed over to our side..."

Spike: "We were always on the same side. For me, the band had a stronger pull than politics or police work."

Sue: "Yes, I think that's what was missing in my life. A sense of purpose and a creative outlet."

Spike: "So that's when we asked Sue if she would like to re-join the band. And we were over the moon when she accepted."

Sue: "Well, playing in front of undercover cops isn't what I set out to do, but we get decent crowds and always get a good reaction. I mean, these people haven't a clue what they're listening to, but they seem to enjoy it."

Spike: "There's something about the lifestyle that you don't get in the force. I think that's why the atmosphere is so good. People can just get into character and be themselves."

Sue: "It is weird being in a pretend band in front of pretend audiences, but that's us I guess. We put the 'nark' into 'anarchy'. Isn't that right Sid?"

Sid: "Yes."

Spike: "He speaks!"

Sid: "Yes I do. And there's something I need to tell you. I haven't been entirely honest with you Spike, Rat, Sue. And it's been eating away at me for years..."

ReCOrd rarities:
Shit ON SOCieTy,
SOCieTY'S LieS EP

In which our protagonist discusses a much sought-after EP, which,
for reasons revealed during the course of the interview, has only
ever been heard by a few people.

First published in One Way Ticket to Cubesville #20 (2017)
RC = Richard Cubesville

Shit on Society were a UK five-piece that even the most eagle-
eyed readers may have missed. After two demos and a few
contributions to compilation cassettes in the early 1980s, they
sank into obscurity. A couple of their members went on to
play in mid-1980s punk/metal crossover bands, but this scene
was eclipsed by the onslaught of UK hardcore, which applied
greater pace and ferocity.

Fast-forward to 2015, when I received an email with a link to
Ebay. Shit on Society's first demo was bought by a Japanese
collector for more than £400 - an astronomical sum for a
home-copied cassette tape whose photocopied cover advised,
"Pay no more than £1-20." A few months later, I came across a
7" single on Discogs, which looked like it contained the two
demos - one on either side. "Funny," says I, "Must be a bootleg."
After all, bands such as Kulturkamf and Godorrhea have made
posthumous vinyl debuts in recent years with demos put to
vinyl by devoted fans. Strangely though, the scant information
on Discogs cited the release date as during the band's brief
existence in 1984.

A chance meeting at the Todmorden zinefair a few months
later provided the final piece to the jigsaw puzzle, when I
mentioned Shit on Society to another stallholder, Liam of Art
Condition Press. His eyes almost popped out of his head, "My

brother-in-law was the original guitarist!" he exclaimed. I
asked him about the single and he told me, yes it does exist,
but no, the songs weren't the original demos; they were re-
recorded. I was by now bursting with curiosity and I begged
Liam to arrange an interview with his brother-in-law, Jon
J. Many thanks to Jon for agreeing to answer my questions,
and hopefully this interview provides readers with valuable
information about a classic "lost band".

RC: Thanks for answering my questions Jon, I appreciate Shit
on Society must be a distant memory now.
JJ: No problem. Hopefully I can clear up a few misconceptions
about Shit on Society. We got a few people's hackles up when we
were around "back in the day", but I don't think people really
understood what we were doing with the band. I think our
music stands the test of time, and I'm really thankful that
people think we're still worth a listen!

RC: Can you give us a potted history of Shit on Society?
JJ: Well, me and Dave Society (drums) were school friends in
Chorley, Lancashire. We were inspired by the punk bands of the
time - Sex Pistols, Clash, Crass, etc, and wanted to start one of
our own. We recruited Nath (bass) from the local youth club
and made the unusual move of adding Gray on synth. I think we
were just looking for any like-minded individuals to form a
band with. I took on vocals, but eventually we met Anton, who
was a natural frontman. Me and Dave Society really wanted the
band to work, but maybe this was our downfall too.

RC: You played only a handful of gigs, was this because there
weren't many venues in Chorley willing to put punk bands on?
JJ: Not really. It soon became obvious to us that Anton was a
troubled lad. He was a great singer, but we didn't communicate
too well. It was difficult to get him to agree to play live,
which for me defeated the point. He'd kind of shut himself off.
I didn't have a problem with Anton, but people started telling
us they were afraid of him.

RC: Tell me about the single - I didn't even know it existed!!
JJ: I've never even listened to it. I know what you're thinking
- this sounds odd! But I saw what it did to Anton, and it
brings back some harsh memories. We recorded two demos in

a period of about three months, and me and Dave Society
were buzzing off them. We got some of the songs released on
compilation tapes, did a few fanzine interviews, and quite a
few people wrote to us. Anton came to the practice one day
and told us he'd got some money, and wanted to self-release a
7" EP. We thought, great! But it sounded a bit sudden. Anton
was insistent that we re-recorded the songs from the demos.
We went into the studio in early 1984, and got all the songs
down in a single day. Not bad for a bunch of inexperienced
kids from Lancashire! Anton then said he wanted to remix the
recording and did his usual disappearing act for a few weeks.

RC: So you never even got to hear the EP?
JJ: Not exactly. Anton reappeared after a while and said the
single was pressed. The change in him was dramatic. He looked
awful, like he hadn't eaten for a long time. And his skin was
really pale, almost opaque. His greasy black hair hung over
his face so we could hardly see it. His voice was shot to pieces
too and he spoke in a low growl that we could hardly hear. I
think Dave Society asked him if he'd been to see a doctor, but
Anton just gave a guttural laugh. It was horrible. After that,
me and Dave Society decided to start another band - Excalibur
Rising. Cheesy I know!! But we were freaked out by Anton and
just wanted to play the music we liked, which at the time was
veering over towards metal.

RC: Did the EP appear?
JJ: After a while, me and Dave Society decided to go round
to Anton's house to see if it had arrived. We'd moved on, but
were curious about it and wanted to put some closure on Shit
on Society. I wish we hadn't. That awful day has haunted my
dreams ever since. I still can't talk about everything we saw.
I don't have the words to describe the abject horror in that
cold, dark house. I'm having a panic attack as I type. We almost
had to hack our way up the overgrown driveway to his mother's
house in Charnock Richard. The overhanging trees blocked
out the light. When we reached the front door, it was cracked
and warped and hung on its hinges. At first we thought Anton
and his mum had been murdered. But what lay behind was much
worse. I pushed open the door and called out for Anton, but
Dave Society put his hand on my arm to stop me. "Jon J! Listen!"
he whispered harshly. I'd never seen Dave Society even ruffled,

115

but I noted the fear in his anguished voice. Somewhere deep
in the house I could hear the opening bars of our song, Not my
Life. But Nath's bassline was distorted out of all recognition
and made my chest pump like I was having a heart attack.
My guitar sounded like... I know it sounds fantastic, but it
sounded like hornets swarming around my head. And then the
deep drumming started and the whole house shook like it was
going to collapse. "Jon J, for Christ's sake let's get out of here,"
Dave Society screamed over the noise. But I was rooted to the
spot. I knew Anton's vocal part came in after Dave Society's
cymbal crash. A blinding light flashed in front of us, through
which we agreed later that we could discern the emaciated
silhouette of Anton as he crept down the stairs towards
our petrified figures. And then the vocal. I have tried to
describe that awful sound afterwards but every time I think
of it my blood freezes. I can only say it was the sound of an
ancient evil intent on the destruction of mankind. It took
what seemed like an age for me to suss that the hysterical
screaming that pierced my eardrums came from my own throat. I
reached out for Dave Society and his face leered close to mine.
His eyes were BLEEDING. I don't know how we escaped from that
hellhouse, but I came round later that cursed night on the
banks of Lower Rivington Reservoir, on a place I recognised as
the site of an ancient burial mound. Dave Society lay corpse-
like beside me. I knew if he ever regained consciousness he
would never regain his sanity too, nor me mine. I watched the
full, hateful, moon rise above the reservoir's black waters and
I cried my eyes out till dawn.

RC: Well thanks for clearing that up Jon. Do you have any plans
for the band?
JJ: We've been asked to play Rebellion festival next year, and
the other members sound quite keen. Fingers crossed for an LP
too. Thanks for the interview mate. Cheers.

OutrO: RePOrt frOm The DePartmeNt Of Lazarus Studies, IaN Dury UNiVerSity Of MusiCOlOgy

"If we think of truth in the early 21st Century," said Professor Atwood at this year's highly popular symposium Music through the Dark Ages, "we have to think of it as being a malleable, constantly shifting concept with no fixed point of reference."

Professor Atwood addressed the gathering during a series of lectures which shared the common theme of Band Reunions by Forgotten People who Slipped Between the Cracks in late 20th and early 21st Century Britain.

This year's event was hosted by Ian Dury University of Musicology's Department of Lazarus Studies. More than 23 academics attended the symposium, with a further 13 joining by telephone. Notes were typed and faxed to all faculty members.

"We have to think of truth as a piece of Plasticine, or modelling clay, in the hands of a child," Professor Atwood continued, "to be bent, twisted and squeezed in all directions before it is finally trampled into the carpet; thus rendering the Plasticine completely useless and ruining the carpet forever. Much to the child's delight and the parents' dismay."

Many of this year's lectures covered the recently discovered text, Killer Tunes and Screaming Bloody Murder in the

Basement of Hell and other stories by Dark Ages author, Cubesville. Little is known about author or text as most information from the Dark Ages - stored electronically - was lost during a time of great upheaval, the internet switch-off (nowadays referred to as The Awakening).

Much has been written about this turbulent era, and the topic is best covered elsewhere (see, for example, Surveillance, Gentrification, and Advertising: Why the internet was sooooo shit, A Felcher [2236]), but unusually for the time, Killer Tunes... was published in paper format and survived The Big Switch-off.

Speaking after their own lecture, The Inedibles: The social and economic conditions for cannibalism under the ravages of capitalism, Dr Ricky Gilead questioned whether Raging Killer Tunes... was truth or fiction, (see also Raging Killer Tunes: Is it a Work of Fiction, or Truth? W Shatner & W Shakespeare, [2287]). This, they added, is immaterial as the text contains valuable clues about the social, economic, ecological and philosophical conditions of the age.

"Unfortunately," Dr Gilead told the assembled musicologists, "it is now popularly believed that groups like Duty, Chaotic Mess, Cthulu Mythos and yes, even Tuesday, were parodies of subcultural music scenes from the time."

During his lecture, Dr Gilead disclosed that the Department of Lazarus Studies had obtained a number of unfinished pieces thought to be by the same author. One bloodthirsty fragment followed a Christmas theme and featured the reunion of a two-piece grindcore band called Anal Fire. Another depicted an early 2000s math metal band called Notified by Email, while a third fragment featured a 1978 Liverpool punk band called The Bootle Urinators. All sadly, said Dr Gilead, fictitious and unfinished.

When asked what he thought these bands would sound like, Dr Gilead turned pale. However, they confided that as with Killer Tunes and Screaming Bloody Murder... the main protagonists in these newly-discovered fragments were anonymous. "Desolation, isolation, alienation," Dr Gilead told the assembled audience, "these were the characteristics of the age. Many of the central characters were overwhelmed by the situations they found themselves in. Their identities were often obscured or eclipsed by the forces of capitalism and most felt a sense of powerlessness; an inability or unwilling to take control of their lives. That's why they got the band back together." Dr Gilead's bold statements were greeted with cries of incredulity and hoots of derision from some sections of the audience.

In reply, Dr Gilead asserted that times before The Awakening were very different from today and many people lacked the self-empowerment that is the cornerstone of modern society. There were, they added some interesting parallels between Dark Age "society" and The Awakening; Dr Gilead cited many characters' anonymity and the common theme of gender fluidity throughout the accounts in Killer Tunes and Screaming Bloody Murder... as important cultural links between the two ages.

The Department of Lazarus Studies has invited papers on next year's theme, "Dead Rock 'n' Rollers: Why couldn't it be [insert name here]?" Interested parties should submit abstracts by the end of the academic year, 31 December.

OTher aNarchO- abSUrdiST WrITiNgS aNd ZiNes bY CubesVille iNCLUde

One Way Ticket to Cubesville zine #1-20
One Way Ticket to Cubesville bumper comp (#21)
One Way Ticket to Cubesville zine #22-24

The Vegan's Guide to People Arguing with Vegans
The Victorian Vegan
The Vegan's Guide to Media Hysteria About Veganism
Veganarchy, Chaos & Destruction #1-2
This is a Zine about Hummus

If the internet still exists when you're reading this, they're probably available through:

https://cubesville.bigcartel.com/

Contact: cubesville@hotmail.com

anarchy & absurdity
since 1987

one way ticket
Cubesville

contact: cubesville@hotmail.com